# Cinderskella

scarily ever laughter
tale 1

For information on subsidiary rights, please contact the publisher at rights@jollyfishpress.com. For a complete list of our wholesalers and distributors, please visit our website at www.jollyfishpress.com. For information, address Jolly Fish Press, PO Box 1773, Provo, UT 84603-1773.
Printed in the United States of America

THIS TITLE IS ALSO AVAILABLE AS AN EBOOK.

Library of Congress Control Number: 2013951267

ISBN 978-1-939967-25-1

10 9 8 7 6 5 4 3 2

scarily ever laughter
tale I

# Cinderskella

## Amie Borst
## Bethanie Borst

illustrated by
Rachael Caringella

JOLLY
**FISH**
PRESS
PROVO, UTAH

Once upon a time in a land far, far away . . . oh, who am I kidding? That's how fairy tales begin, and my story is anything but a fairy tale; it's true.

It was a cold day in February and quite possibly the worst day of my life. I would say it sucked (because for most people it would, especially if they're only eleven and three-quarters like me), but if I did, my dad would give me a look. You know, the one that says, *If parents could still wash their children's mouths out with soap, I'd scrub your tongue with a bar of Dial.* So, instead, I'll just say it was awful.

I sat at my desk in Mrs. Femur's sixth grade science class, taking notes from the board, completely minding my own business. As I always do. Except for that time I nosed into Vicki Larson's science project, but that doesn't count since she asked me to help. I can't help it if I'm not a professional science person. What did she expect? I mean, it's not like I knew the thing would explode. Besides, what's so important about the skeletal system anyway? It's just bones. We've all got them.

I glanced around the room, watching my classmates and realized something. Even though middle school started off pretty cool, it really wasn't any different than elementary school. Teachers still nagged for assignments. Boys still acted stupid thinking they looked cool, and girls were still desperately trying to get their attention. Then there was Principal Petto (with his nasty-looking comb-over), who was a lot like my last principal. He paced the halls as if his sole purpose in life was to make us miserable. Rumor had it he was nice, long ago, when he was the shop teacher, carving wood and collecting shavings. But becoming principal turned him sour, like a little boy without his candy.

Ethan McCallister strode into the room and sat across from me. My heart leapt a little. Maybe it was his wavy brown hair. Or the way a little dimple appeared in his right cheek whenever he smiled. He turned and made googly eyes at Vicki Larson and I wondered why he never seemed to notice me.

It was time to commence with Operation Lip Balm, a.k.a. Operation Chapstick because, once I looked in my backpack, I realized that was all I had.

I smeared a heavy line of cherry-flavored Chapstick across my lips. Then, I smacked them loudly for dramatic effect. I stood up really slowly, making my back as straight as a supermodel's. Even my legs did the supermodel walk, crisscrossing in front of me as I approached the head of the room. Ethan was for sure going to notice me!

I strutted past him, puckering my lips so I looked all pouty, because that's what the magazines portray as awesomeness. I knew I looked mega "kewl" because everyone stared at me. My supermodel crossed-legged walk was a hit!

Mrs. Femur tipped her head. "Cindy, do you need to use the restroom?" The lenses of her cat-eye shaped glasses reflected the ceiling lights, casting a glare on her eyes. It made me stare at her, trying to figure out why she would ask such a crazy question.

"Uh, no, I, um . . . need to sharpen my pencil."

"Don't you think you need a pencil in order to do that?" Mrs. Femur pushed her glasses back.

"A pencil?" Shoot. This wasn't working out the way I'd planned. I would just have to go back to my desk, get a pencil, and do my super strut again. Then Ethan would notice me. Twice!

On my way back, I lucked out. Ethan was watching me! Unfortunately, I paid too much attention to him—smiling so wide my cherry-flavored lips stuck to my teeth—and not enough attention to my untied shoelace. I tripped. Then I fell. In slow motion. "I'm faaaalllliiiinnngggg . . ." I said, even though I didn't mean to say it out loud.

Everyone laughed. Every. One. Including Ethan.

The worst part? Ethan's face changed from a huge dimpled smile, his laughter echoing in the whole room, to an expression of *Oh, no!*

The *worser* than worst part? I landed right on Ethan's desk, smacking his face with my fist in the process. That was probably why his face looked so scared. Blood gushed everywhere.

"Omygosh! Cindy gave Ethan a bloody nose!" someone yelled.

Ethan looked at me, horrified. He touched a finger to his nose, saw the blood running onto his palm, and raced out of the room.

I guess I managed to get his attention this time, even if it wasn't exactly the way I'd hoped.

Mrs. Femur pointed to a boy on the other side of the room. "Hurry and follow Ethan to the nurse, please. Make sure he's all right." Then she cleared her throat. "As soon as Cindy takes a seat, we'll get started."

"Looks like she already took one," Vicki Larson said. It was so funny I forgot to laugh. Face flushing hot, I rolled off Ethan's desk and crawled back into my own seat.

The teacher babbled on in science talk while I gazed at the empty desk on my left. If only my BFF Sarah would hurry home from her vacation. She had been gone for, like, ever and I really missed our girl talk and master plans on how to nab Ethan. Obviously, my latest attempt was an epic fail. Tripping in front of the entire class and falling into him wasn't exactly what I'd had in mind. And my previous attempts (Operation Bathroom Stakeout, Mission Mascara, and Task Force TOO-Skinny Jeans) only resulted in a toilet paper-covered shoe, a black-smeared nightmare, and a rip in the butt of my pants.

Mr. G. Petto, a.k.a the super-enthusiastic, woodcarving

shop teacher turned overbearing school Nazi, buzzed in on the class intercom. "Mrs. Femur?"

"Yes?"

The class broke out in a chorus of hisses and oohs. There were even a few chuckles. Great. I was in trouble. The last thing I wanted was a visit with Mr. Comb-over. Dad didn't need the stress of another mess up. Not now. Not while . . .

"Settle down." Mrs. Femur glared at us, placing a finger to her lips. "Class. Hush!"

"Can you hear me?"

Mrs. Femur wiped her brow. "Yes, yes, I can hear you."

Principal Petto cleared his throat. "Good, good. Um, if you would, please have Cindy pack up." He sounded nervous and it made my stomach drop to the floor like it does when I'm on a roller coaster.

It seemed everyone turned around at once and stared at me. "Oooooh . . . Cindy's in trouble!" I heard someone hum from the back of the room. But that's not what made me feel sick. I knew it was something much worse than being in trouble.

"She needs to go home . . . for the day," the principal finished. It wasn't his voice that grated on my nerves worse than Vicki's "googly" eyes at Ethan, but the words he said.

It really shouldn't have been a surprise. I knew it was coming.

Still, I didn't want to go home. I knew what waited for me there.

## chapter 2

After I checked out of the office, I headed home. Dad wouldn't dare leave to pick me up.

My chest ached. I didn't want to face what lay ahead, so I dragged my feet hoping that would make my worries go away. I wished the six-block walk were twenty, and that the row houses were country homes, each with ten acres of land instead of little postage stamp lots.

When I reached the house, a single light shone in the upstairs window. Despite its glow, the house seemed dark and gloomy. I longed for school and my friends.

Anything but home.

Once I pushed through the front door, I knew where to find him. I climbed the stairs, one at a time, my heart pounding in my chest, my stomach in my throat. I'd never felt so sick in all my life. Maybe I didn't have to face this. It wouldn't be that horrible if I turned in the other direction and headed back to school. There was still time. And maybe—just maybe—there might be something I could do to change this . . . make it better . . .

Dad stood in the doorway of Mom's room, his arms crossed tightly over his chest.

I stared at him, hoping that if we locked eyes long enough, it wouldn't be true. He'd smile, tell me it was a false alarm, to go back to school. Be with my friends.

After a long moment—my palms sweating, throat aching—Dad stepped forward. "It's time, Cindy." He motioned for me, waving his hand in the direction of her bed.

No! Not those words! I'd been dreading hearing them. Even though Mom had been sick for a while, it seemed like this day came way too fast. It was just yesterday that we were watching movies and laughing. Only the other day she walked me to school and I acted embarrassed, even though secretly I was glad she was there. Because middle school was scary. Or so I thought. What I was about to face was a whole lot scarier.

The smell hit me like a wall when I entered Mom's room. It was like a bunch of old people had decided to move in, a mixture of herbs and medicines floating in the air. I sat on the edge of her bed and kissed her moist cheek. Beads of sweat formed a line on her upper lip.

"I love you, Cindy," she said as she stroked my hair with a sweaty palm. The smell of her perfume so faint it almost wasn't there. I wondered how long before she'd fade away, too, and I'd forget her altogether. Her voice garbled and cracked like she was in a lot of pain. "You be strong for me."

I didn't want to hear it. Not goodbye. Not that it was over. None of it. "Don't worry." I brushed a strand of her soft brown hair from her face. "Everything's going to be all right. You're going to be okay."

It was a lie. I knew nothing would be all right, and that she wouldn't be okay. She was dying, which meant she'd never be with me anymore. There would be no more singing funny songs (most of them about Dad) or playing games, and there'd be no more late nights telling stories. There'd be no more watching scary movies huddled under a blanket together. There'd be no more . . .

Mom's weak arm gave way and dropped on my lap. She gently gripped my hand and patted it. "Promise you'll be good." Her voice was so small, fading away. Just like her. "My dear little Cinderella."

A small smile pulled at my lips. Even though I wasn't little anymore, and I definitely wasn't a princess, I didn't mind hearing the nickname again because it would probably be the last time. My dad would never call me Cinderella. I was his "Lovie." The princess thing was all Mom.

"I'll always be with you," Mom said. "You know that. Right?" I could see it took every ounce of everything Mom had left to utter those words, her frail body shivering, her lips hardly moving.

I nodded. "Uh-huh." After swallowing hard, I said, "Always." But I knew she wouldn't. I could feel her disappearing all ready. She'd be gone and I'd forget her, no matter how hard I tried to hold on. My chest ached as I held back a sob.

Mom grunted as she lifted her hand and placed it on my face. She stroked her thumb across my cheek, closed her eyes, and hummed out a bunch of words I couldn't understand. It almost sounded like a chant of some sort.

Dad ran into the room, stumbling over his own feet. "No! Tabitha!" He reached for my mom's hands. The desperation on his face scared me and I wanted to stop him, but froze. "You promised."

Mom gazed at Dad. "Please forgive me, Roger." Her face scrunched up like a rotten apple as she fought hard not to cry. But a tear escaped anyway and rolled down her cheek.

My gaze darted between the two of them. I grabbed Mom's hand, squeezing tight—an uneasiness settling in the room. "Forgive you? For what?" A strange feeling sank to the pit of my stomach. It was like millions of needles in my belly were doing acrobatics, making me want to vomit. But I didn't.

Dad sat on the edge of the bed, holding his face. "You promised, you promised," he whispered, shaking his head. "It's too dangerous. Someone will find out."

Mom smiled weakly and fluttered her eyes. Then she let out a soft breath. Her face looked so peaceful I knew she was gone.

I threw my arms around her. "Mom! No! Don't go." My voice came out broken, just like my heart. I put my head to her chest and cried. Well, actually, I sobbed.

### *TIME OUT!*

*First of all, no, I'm not a baby. Second of all, you know all that stuff they say about being strong? Well, that stuff is stupid. No one is so strong that they don't cry when someone they love dies. And if they are, then there's something seriously wrong with them. Seriously.*

Dad pulled me up and hugged me. I squeezed him once in return, then pushed away. Tears streaked my face as I ran to my room. My mom was dead and gone, and I knew she'd never be with me anymore. It was over. There was no love in death. Death was blackness and misery. And forgetting.

A mixture of sadness and anger flooded my chest, making my insides burn. All I wanted to do was sleep. Forever. Just like Mom.

Pastor Stan arrived moments later. He stood in the doorway wearing a black suit. One arm cradled a book, the other he used to run a hand through his slicked back hair. Dad motioned for him to come in and they stood there wordlessly for a long time. The pastor led Dad into the kitchen, where they sat at the table. I couldn't hear what they were saying, but as soon as I saw Dad's shoulders heaving, I covered my ears to block out his sobs.

I must have fallen asleep because I woke up to a houseful of people. The funeral director and a few men in dark suits took Mother's body away on a stretcher, and our house immediately felt like something was missing, empty. But worse, it made me feel like a piece of my heart was gone. Our house and my heart were nothing more than a shell.

Dad spent most of the remainder of the day on the phone and I wandered to my room and slept in bed.

Well, I tried to sleep, but all I did was toss and turn. I longed for the feeling of Mom's arms wrapped around me, but instead my bed poked me with its uncomfortable springs. Plus, my stomach was on fire and all my bones felt like they would explode.

Days passed and on the afternoon of the funeral, I marched to the closet and pulled out a black dress. *Perfect.* It was just what I'd seen people in movies wear to funerals, plus it matched my mood. Miserable.

My head throbbed as I walked as slowly as possible, dragging my feet all the way down the stairs. Dad stood by the front door in his best pinstriped suit. He wore Mom's favorite red tie, the one with the whimsical gold swirls. "You look better."

I gave him a look. It said, *My stomach feels like a thousand snakes are squirming inside it, my bones ache, I lost my mom, and you think I look better?*

Dad stretched out his hand to mine. "C'mon. The limo's waiting."

I nodded, reaching back, letting his large, strong hands swallow mine. All I could do was squeeze his hand because if I said anything I'd either break down and cry or throw something and watch it smash into a gazillion tiny little pieces. I would have been okay with that, though I think Dad would have been a bit peeved.

The limo driver, in his freshly-pressed navy suit with gold buttons, held the door open for us. Then he drove super slowly. Like so slowly I could have walked to the services.

At the church the organ music pounded in my ears. Pastor Stan shook Dad's hand. Then he bent down to me. "I'm so sorry for your loss."

It wasn't long before the church filled with Mom's friends. There were a lot of handshakes, head tips, and sad-eye looks. Once everyone was seated, the organist finally stopped playing the loud, irritating music. Pastor Stan took his place at the pulpit and gave a speech. Then, other people got up and shared all their stories about my mom.

Hours passed as I stared at the stained glass image behind the pastor, trying to block out all the talks, tears, and sobs. Reliving memories wasn't my idea of fun. What I really wanted was my mom with me to make more memories.

Finally, the service ended and everyone filed out the door. Dad put his arm around me. "C'mon, kiddo." He handed me a bouquet of daisies from the pulpit. "For the grave," he said. Then he led me to the limo.

At the cemetery, they lowered Mom's casket into the ground. With each inch, I felt like a piece of my soul died. Pastor Stan said a prayer and tossed a handful of dirt on top of the casket.

Rain sprinkled from the sky and I clenched the daisies in my hand even tighter. Mom's two favorite things were daisies and rainstorms.

"It never rains in February," someone whispered.

They were right. Not in New York. Snow maybe, but never rain. Still, I was too upset to care.

### *TIME OUT!*

*This is called foreshadowing. If you don't know what that is, ask your teacher. She'll explain it. Or ask the kid sitting next to you. The one picking his nose. Hmmm . . . on second thought, never mind. DO NOT ask him. In fact, you should probably ask your teacher if you can move your desk. Preferably across the room.*

The rain came down heavier, soaking the mourners. "Leave the flowers," Dad said, urging me to place them on the ground.

But I ignored him and just stood there in the pouring rain, staring at the hole in the ground where my mom would stay forever. I watched as the water puddled around my feet and raced its way into the grave, splashing as it hit the casket. It didn't bother me that my shoes were covered in mud or that I was drenched. Because I hardly felt anything. I was too numb.

As I watched the water splash onto the casket and rush into the soil, white vines grew around the coffin. *That's odd.* Maybe some of the petals from the daisies had dropped in there.

I stretched out my arm, reaching for them. Maybe Mom was trying to talk to me. Maybe she wanted one last moment together. My heart ached for it, too.

The vines grew rapidly, surrounding the casket and dragging it farther into the earth. *No, no, no!* I wasn't ready to let her go. Nothing was going to drag her into the ground!

Desperate, I fell to my knees and leaned in closer. As I reached my hand toward the vines, they paused as if they were aware of me. They turned slowly, tilting in my direction. I felt my eyes grow wide as the white vines sprouted faster, climbing the walls, twisting and twining around each other until they became creepy, gnarled skeleton hands.

I glanced around at the people surrounding me. Everyone just stood there, completely unaware. They had no idea that my mom's casket was about to be dragged into the ground by creepy white skeleton hands. I had to do something—had to stop it. I turned back toward the casket, leaned over the edge, and peered into the hole. The vines shot out of the ground and lunged at me.

A scream caught in my throat as I flew backward.

"Cindy." Dad knelt down and wrapped his arms around me. His scratchy wool suit made my face itch. "I'm so sorry."

There was an ache in my stomach, a fire in my chest. "Mom—casket—"

"I know it's hard, Lovie. But she's gone. You have to let her go." He stroked my hair, as if it would bring me some form of comfort.

"But the . . . the . . ." I broke away from Dad to look into the hole in the ground. "The casket."

My eyes felt blurry—maybe because of tears, maybe because I couldn't believe what I saw—so I rubbed my palms against them. When I looked at the grave again every-thing was exactly the same as when Pastor Stan said his prayer. The skeleton hands were gone. The white vines had disappeared.

There was just Mom's casket with my bouquet of daisies on top.

chapter 3

**D**ad wrapped his coat around my shoulders, the smell of damp wool invaded my nose, making me sick. He led me to the limo. The ride home passed in a blur. It all seemed like a bad dream I desperately wanted to wake up from.

Still drenched, I went to my room and collapsed on my bed. I lay there and wished my mom wasn't gone. And I wished all the people downstairs—the ones who came from the funeral bringing casseroles and biscuits, pies, and cookies—would just go home.

"I brought you a brownie, sugah," said Ms. Wanda Fey, the nice old lady who lived next door. She sat on the edge of my bed, the mattress sinking beneath her weight. "And a glass of moo-moo juice." She placed the treats on my nightstand, her smooth, dark skin reminded me of Dad's morning coffee.

I sat up, rubbing my eyes. "Moo-moo juice?"

Ms. Wanda gave a chuckle. "Nice, warm milk. Perfect for an upset tummy." She put her arm around my shoulder, but I felt myself tense. How did she know my stomach had been hurting for days? "Now you better eat that brownie, Miss Cindy. You know what they say about chocolate, don't you?"

I shook my head.

"Well, I'll be! Never heard it?"

I shook my head again.

"Chocolate heals what ails you." She took my hands in hers, giving them a pat. Ms. Wanda (who insisted I call her by her first name because she said being called Mrs. Fey made her feel old) had a way of cheering up just about anyone with her southern charm.

"Don't know if you can go believing all those wives' tales or not." She gave a broad laugh. "But it sure does make me feel better." She rubbed her belly. "Heaven knows I don't need it!"

I nodded. But I couldn't eat.

Ms. Wanda sat quietly for a minute, looking in my eyes. "I'll let ya be, sugah." She squeezed me before leaving the room and added, "You need something—well, you just pick up that phone and call me. You hear?" Her kindness made me realize how much I needed my BFF, Sarah. But since she was on vacation, she probably didn't even know my mom died. She hadn't called. Probably because she was having too much fun.

With tears rolling down my cheeks, I curled into a ball. The voices of all the guests dwindled until only silence remained. The moon cast a soft glow in my room and I fell asleep.

My stomach did this achy bubbly thing and I sat up, covering my mouth with my hands. I raced into my private bathroom on the other side of my bedroom and threw up. A lot. Like more than I ever thought possible. Maybe I should have drunk that moo-moo juice Ms. Wanda had given me.

I felt like one of those dead animal carcasses they have to scrape off the road, so I sat on the tile floor next to my bathtub and moaned.

"Cindy," I heard dad call from the hallway, knocking on my bedroom door. "Are you all right, Lovie?"

I left the bathroom and tried to crawl to my bedroom door but it seemed to get farther and farther away. When I finally reached the handle, breathless and weak, I stood up and opened the door a crack. "Just fine," I said trying to sound like I hadn't been sick, which was really hard because my throat was all scratchy. My voice sounded like sandpaper on metal.

"Do you need anything?" Dad tried to peek into my room, but I hid behind the door so he couldn't see how sick I was.

"No. I'm . . . I'm fine," I lied.

Dad took a deep breath. "Go back to bed. I'm sure you'll feel better in the morning." I quickly glanced into the hall, careful not to let him see me, and caught a glimpse of his face as he turned away. He looked a tad twitchy, but I figured he must just be sad about Mom, too.

"I'm sure I will." I closed the door behind me and leaned against the frame. When the hall light went out, I walked, half-hunched and slower than an old lady, to my bed. The covers were in the way; moving them took too much energy, so I just collapsed on top of them.

Before long, my stomach churned again and I sat bolt upright in my bed. I vomited all over my favorite blanket. The one Mom had made for my third birthday.

I picked up my blanket, stumbling back into my bathroom. If I could hide the blanket in my bathtub, I knew I'd be safe from Dad finding it. He didn't have to know I'd gotten sick again.

Dad knocked on my door. "Cindy," he called.

I quickly dropped the blanket in the tub, raced over to my door, and straightened myself, determined not to look sick. Then I slowly opened the door and peeked through the small crack.

"You okay?" But before I could answer, he pushed the door open the rest of the way. "Oh, my." He did this little gasp thing, sucking in his breath on the word "oh," and I knew the "my" was just to cover it all up. His mouth fell open wide. His eyes grew ten times their normal size, like a goldfish with those bug-out eyes. Dad backed away, muttering, "Uh, uh, uh."

"What?" I looked around my room, hoping whatever hideous thing that shocked my father wouldn't scare me, too. "What's the matter?"

"Don't worry, Cindy." He reached out his hand like he

wanted to pat me on the head, but he paused, then slowly withdrew. "You'll be just fine in the morning." As Dad closed the door, he mumbled under his breath. It was something about Mom. Something about a curse. And something about it being worse than he imagined.

*A curse?* My brain was too foggy to think straight. Dad couldn't have said that. I was definitely hearing things. Mom hadn't used magic in years. Not since she graduated from GWU (Green Witch University—though she told everyone else she'd gone to George Washington University) long before I was born. In fact, I didn't know anybody who used magic. But this was New York—anything was possible. I mean, have you ever seen a Broadway show? Pure magic.

In my bed, snuggled under a clean blanket, I stared at the ceiling. But all I could see was my dad's face, his eyes all bugged out, his mouth open so wide he could catch flies. The thought of my dad like that made me restless.

*Think of something else—anything else.*

That night I dreamt of my mom dancing with skeletons. Cackling skeletons, menacing skeletons, and creeping skeletons. They pranced around my room and laughed.

Even though I should probably have been irritated that the sun shone in my room all bright and chipper-like, it actually made me feel better. Plus, my stomach wasn't achy anymore. It seemed pointless to mope in my room, so I went downstairs. Dad was in the kitchen cooking. He handed me a plate of scrambled eggs. He was the best cook. Ever.

### TIME OUT!

*Yes. My dad can cook. Besides, I had thrown up like the entire contents of my stomach, so even if his food tasted like something from the school cafeteria's garbage bin, I'm sure I wouldn't have cared.*

"Feeling better this morning?"

"Yeah. All better," I said, stuffing a spoonful of fluffy eggs into my mouth.

Dad smiled. "I see your appetite is back." He turned away and scrambled another egg in the pan. "The school called." His voice got quiet and I knew he was really just sad about Mom. "They're sending your work home for a while. Just until you've adjusted." He cleared his throat. "I mean, until you're ready to go back."

I couldn't open my mouth to say anything because I knew if I did, I'd just cry. There went my good mood. So, I choked back my tears, my throat feeling like fire, and nodded.

While Dad washed dishes I went to the family room and flicked on the TV. I flipped through the channels, but it was all cartoons and talk shows.

I sat by the front window and watched the snow fall. The weather was an emotional wreck lately, kind of like me. It wasn't really unusual for New York to have weird weather. Even still, rain on my mother's funeral, then snow today was a bit much. The snow stuck, too, covering the ground in white, reminding me of the inside of a snow globe.

The sound of the phone ringing stole my thoughts. Since Dad was still washing dishes, I figured I ought to answer it.

"Uh, hello."

"Sugah? It's Ms. Wanda," Her sweet southern voice sang like a bell. "I'm just checking on ya'll. What you in need of?"

I wanted to say, *"I need my mom. And my best friend."* But instead, I said, "We don't need anything, thank you. We're fine."

"Well, I'm right next door, sugah, if you change your mind."

"Okay."

"Just you remember; sometimes magic comes from the most unexpected places."

"Um. Sure. Thanks. Bye." I hung up the phone before my voice got wonky trying to hold back my tears.

I climbed the stairs feeling like a slug. All the energy was sucked from my body, a trail of slime followed wherever I went. (Well, okay, that didn't really happen, but at least it would have been interesting.) I went to my room thinking about Ms. Wanda's words. What did she know about magic? Maybe she'd lived in New York too long and she was becoming weird like the rest of us. Or it was probably just her way of saying I'd feel better soon.

That night, I woke up again. If history was going to repeat itself, I knew I'd need to visit the porcelain god. So I walked across my room to my bathroom. Still groggy-eyed, I flipped on the light and turned on the faucet, letting the water run.

I splashed the water on my face, but I couldn't tell if it was hot or cold. In fact, I couldn't really even feel the water at all. There was a fresh towel by the sink. I grabbed it and patted my face dry. When I finished, I put the towel back on the rack and turned to look at myself in the mirror. That was when I saw exactly what had made my father's eyes grow so wide and his mouth to drop open.

I was a skeleton.

Yep.

A boney, white skeleton.

## chapter 4

**M**y brain went crazy with thoughts. But the one that stuck out was this: *HELP! I've been skin-napped!*

### *TIME OUT!*

*See? I told you this wasn't a fairy tale. I mean, how many fairy tales have you read where a girl turns into a skeleton? Plus, most fairy tales were written by creepy dead guys. (Okay, they weren't dead when they wrote the stories, but they're dead now—hey, I wonder if that makes them kind of like zombies.) Anyway, they probably didn't like girls much because they always made them kiss frogs and beasts. I mean, what kind of sick person kisses frogs anyway? So, yeah, since this is true and not written by a dead guy, I've got those stories beat by a long shot.*

A scream burst through my mouth. A hot stream of terror ran through my body—kind of like it did all those times I watched scary movies with Mom. But this was much different from a movie because this was *real!*

No! This had to be a horrible nightmare. Stuff like this just didn't happen. Not to me.

I tried to blink my eyes but without eyelids, they just rolled around in my head. That was helpful. *Not.*

Wait. I was a skeleton . . . with eyeballs? *Weird.*

This was the strangest dream ever. There was only one other way to wake myself from this craziness. So I rolled up the sleeve of my pajamas and gripped one of the bones in my arm and squeezed. But I couldn't very well pinch bone since my fingers slipped off. It was kind of impossible.

Which meant this wasn't a dream at all!

"Dad!" I screamed as I stood in my bathroom, looking at myself—or what remained of myself—in the mirror. "Daaa-aaad." This time my voice went up too high.

Dad ran into my room so quickly he lost his footing as he turned the corner and he did this catapult-like move where half his body went one way and the other half went the other. If I hadn't been so freaked out about the pajama-wearing skeleton reflection in the mirror, I probably would have laughed.

"What's the matter, Cin—" he started to say but then he caught a glimpse of me in the mirror. "Oh. Oh," he said and his voice did that little thing where he sucked in air on his first "oh," but there was no "my" to cover it up this time; just another "oh" that sounded like he released his air.

"What is that?" I pointed at the reflection in the mirror.

"Well, it looks like it's a skeleton," Dad said. His voice didn't comfort me. It was plain. Matter-of-fact.

"B-b-but w-w-w?" I tried, unsuccessfully, not to stutter.

"I do believe it's you."

"Of course, it's me," I said trying to give *him* a look, one that would say, *Well duh, who else would it be?* But without skin and eyebrows, nothing changed on my face. It was just all . . . bone. "But why?" I asked. "I mean, how?"

Dad shrugged. "Dunno, kiddo." He used his silly rhyming voice, then scratched his head, then his arm, and then his face. And that was when I knew he wasn't telling the truth because he always gets all twitchy and nervous when he's trying to hide something.

"Not a good time for rhymes, Dad. I'm kind of, like, a skeleton here!"

"Sorry, Lovie." He reached out his hand to pat my head again, but he withdrew like he did before.

That was when I started to feel really bad. As if being a skeleton wasn't enough, it was like my dad was afraid of me or something, and it made me feel horrible. I started to cry, except there were no tears, just the sound of my voice breaking into sobs.

"It's going to be all right," Dad said. "We'll find a way out of this. I promise."

I nodded. Then Dad walked me back to bed and tucked me in, but he didn't kiss me goodnight.

When morning came, I sat up with a start. *Please let me be normal.* I threw back the covers, my heart racing.

Feet. Normal feet!

I pulled up my sleeves. Hands and arms. With skin!

I raced into the bathroom, smiling at my reflection. "I'm normal! I'm Cindy!" I shouted as I danced around the room. "Dad!"

Dad skidded into the room, bringing a tray of breakfast food with him, nearly spilling the orange juice on the way. "What is it?"

"I'm normal! I'm not a skeleton anymore!"

Dad smiled weakly.

That was when I realized that he knew. He knew all along! I plopped on the bed in disbelief. He'd kept a secret from me. I glared at him because there was no way I would let him off the hook so easily. "You knew about this? Why didn't you tell me? I mean, didn't it occur to you that I might need to know I was a skeleton?" I asked (actually, it probably sounded more like a demand because it felt demanding when I said it).

Dad shook his head. "I didn't know how." He sat on the edge of my bed, balancing the tray on his lap, a solemn mood settling on us. "Besides, would you have believed me if I did?"

I shrugged, realizing he was right. "Probably not."

Dad's sad eyes looked into mine. "Your mom . . ." he said, his voice trailing off. He didn't need to finish the sentence.

I twiddled with the corner of my blanket. "I know." When I was sure my voice wouldn't crack, I said, "She loved me. You don't have to say it." Then I stared into his eyes, forcing

Amie & Bethanie Borst

myself to be strong when what I really wanted was to tell him how much I missed her. Everything bubbled up in my chest. But I shot my gaze to the tray of food. There were pancakes and bacon and a glass of orange juice. It looked so yummy my mouth started to water.

Dad shook his head. "I don't think you understand."

"Understand what?"

There was this awkward moment of silence where we both just looked at each other funny. Then he said, "That your mom did this to you."

"I'm a skeleton because of her?" My voice got tight on the last word. But somehow, deep inside, I kind of knew she had done this to me. How else could something so freaky happen? I was pretty sure neither of us knew *why* she had done it. Or maybe Dad did know, and that was just another thing he was keeping from me. I sat up straight and stared him in the eyes. "But why? Why would she do this to me?"

Dad looked away.

"What do you know about this?" I said, my voice giving him that *I know you know something, mister* tone.

Dad's shoulders went up as he inhaled. This was it! He was going to tell me. Dad let out his breath, turned back to me and smoothed my hair. "Eat up. When you're finished we can do whatever you want today."

That was it? He wasn't going to tell me? I crossed my arms and huffed. "I don't want to do anything," I said, my voice choking on tears. Mom was gone and I missed her so much my chest ached. I couldn't ask her why she would do something like this to me and she wasn't around to help me figure it out. And oh, yeah, I was a skeleton. Well, only at night, but still, I was a freaky skeleton.

Even though I was normal-Cindy this morning, I didn't know if the curse would change. Maybe it would start happening during the day, too! My palms got sweaty at the thought. What would my friends think of me? Did they even like skeletons? After Vicki Larson's skeleton explosion, I wasn't sure.

What bothered me the most, though, was that my dad felt repulsed by me, and I didn't know how I would learn to live with such an awful thing. I was a monster. And I didn't want to be a monster. I wanted to be a normal almost-twelve-year-old middle-schooler.

"Well, when you're ready to do something, I'll be here," Dad said.

But after breakfast, I wasn't ready to do something. After lunch, I wasn't ready to do something. And after dinner I went to bed and cried myself to sleep. Which was a good thing. At least I wouldn't have to deal with being a skeleton. I could sleep right through it.

I dreamt of my mom. She stood by her headstone. "Ciiiiin-dyyyyy," she called in a low, soft singsong voice. "Come viiiiiis-it me." White vines grew around her feet, twisted around her body, then shot out at me.

I sat up with a start and looked around the room—half creeped out, half excited about the vision of my mom. Somehow, it made me feel like she was near. "Mom? Are you there?" I whispered. But there was no response.

My brain thought about the creepy white vines, which

reminded me of the whole freaky-skeleton-girl thing. I wished I'd been able to stay asleep, but maybe my fate changed this time. So, I got out of bed, went to the bathroom, turned on the light, and looked in the mirror. The reflection of a skeleton stared back at me. I felt desperate. And pathetic. There was no doubt now. This was my curse forever and ever.

"Why did you do this to me?" I whispered. "What kind of mom would do such a horrible thing?"

My sobs grew louder and louder, but Dad never came to my room. It was like he gave up on me or something. But it didn't matter because there wasn't anything to say. Nothing could make this better and nothing would make it go away.

### TIME OUT!

*Don't start crying on me. Please. Seriously, don't. Oh, good grief, I'll wait while you go get yourself a tissue . . . (Waits patiently), (taps pencil), (looks at watch), (wonders why you haven't moved your desk yet because that kid is still picking his nose) . . . All better? Good.*

When I woke up the next morning, I showered, dressed, and raced downstairs. Dad lay on the couch but I walked right past him, straight to the kitchen and grabbed a granola bar. Then I put on my coat and boots and left. Without saying a single word. If he wasn't going to tell me anything, I was determined to find out for myself. I didn't care if he was angry or if I'd be grounded. There wasn't any punishment worse than being a skeleton.

I ran. I ran so fast my lungs felt like they were on fire. I kept running, past the houses and the stores, straight to the cemetery. Black swirly letters formed the words *Parkview Cemetery* across the tall iron fence.

My lungs gasping for air, I stared at those gates, hating that they kept me out, away from my mom. Angrily, I slammed my hands against them, the black iron icy cold. The gates creaked open.

A flutter tickled my chest. Was I really going to do this?

Yes. I had to. I had no choice.

Determined, I trudged through the snow. My boots absorbed the slushy late winter snow, the chill seeping in straight to my toes. Still, I pressed forward through the cemetery, down the rows of headstones, trying my best to remember the exact spot of Mom's gravesite.

Wind whipped around me, my hair tangling into a knotty mess. I snuggled into my coat, trying to keep warm. My nose dripped, eyes watered. Fighting the wind and snow through tears, I finally spotted her headstone. I knew it was hers because it was the only one that was pure white. All the others were just shades of gray.

My step quickened, a rush filling me. I didn't know if I wanted to tell her how angry I was or throw myself on her grave and beg her to come back. She had done such an awful thing to me. But deep down I hoped that maybe there was a reason for it. My mom would never do something so horrible without a purpose.

"Well, Mom. I'm here."

There was no response.

"You told me to come visit."

Still nothing.

"Why did you want me here? So you could laugh at what you did?" I stood there in the cold wind, fighting tears and anger, my hands balled into tight fists, and my teeth clenched.

Nothing.

"So you could tell me you missed me?"

A strong wind whipped around the headstone, blowing flakes of fresh snow into the air. The flakes floated, drifting until they formed into the figure of a skeleton hand. It lunged at me, its boney fingers reaching out, like they were trying to grip me by the throat.

Backing away, my feet slipped on an icy patch and I lost my balance, falling on the grave. White vines grew from the earth, slithering around my body like little snakes. They wrapped around my belly, tying me to the earth. *No. No, this wouldn't be happening!* My heart pounded. Trapped, I flailed in the mushy snow, my arms waving and my legs kicking.

"No, no, no!" I screamed. A vine slithered across my mouth, muffling my cries. Another one twisted around an arm, then a leg. I had to break free. Those weeds weren't going to drag me into the ground!

chapter 5

"Cindy, it's just me," Dad said. He had an arm around my middle, hugging me tight. "Calm down," he soothed, rocking me in his arms.

### TIME OUT!

*I know. It's crazy, right? How do parents always know where we are, even when we don't want them to? You could pack a bag and run away (but I don't advise doing that—I tried it once and let's just say the rats in the subway are definitely bigger when you're by yourself), and yet, like magic, they find you. Maybe that's not such a bad thing after all. Look what would have happened if Dad hadn't found me. I would have been dragged into the ground with corpses and bugs and creepy dead stuff. Gross!*

I blinked. I was still in the cemetery but there weren't any vines—not on my mouth, not on my arm or leg, or around my stomach. It was just my dad's loving arms. There wasn't any floating snow in the shape of a skeleton hand. I rubbed my eyes and looked at my dad. He had an expression on his face. It said, *I'm sorry this has been so hard on you.*

"C'mon now." Dad helped me up. "Let's get home before you catch a cold."

My clothes were covered in slushy, wet snow. My fingers and toes were like ice cubes. "Too late," I said shivering.

After a hot bath, warm pajamas—straight from the dryer, just like Mom used to do—and a bowl of chicken noodle soup, I felt much better.

Even though Dad made some great attempts, things were still awkward. Would he ever accept me? The new, skeleton me? Would I ever be comfortable with myself and my new skin? Or lack of it, more like.

The day passed to night and my body tingled. That was the first sign that triggered my skeleton transformation. My skin glowed softly, became translucent, and vanished.

Maybe Mom wanted me to visit my memories of her and not her grave, so I remembered all the ways she'd helped me get over feeling sorry for myself when bad stuff happened. Like the time when I was four and I lost my favorite doll. She played with me for hours. It helped me forget about my doll. Or when I spilled paint on my favorite jeans. She brought me on a shopping spree. Or when my cat, Scruffy, died. Mom rocked me in her arms and cried, too. Without fail, Mom would say, "It's all about your attitude, Cindy."

Even though I was still scared about what had happened at the cemetery, I had to do something. Anything to make my situation better.

So that was what I did. I changed my attitude.

I stood in front of the mirror and patted my face. "You can get through this," I said. "It's just temporary. A phase." I didn't know how much good my mini-pep talk was doing because I really didn't feel any different, but I figured it couldn't hurt anything.

I'm pretty sure it didn't help much at all because looking at my reflection still made me feel funny. I wasn't pretty Cindy with a head full of golden hair. Nope, I was freaky Cindy with a skull full of bone.

But I kept at it because I really wanted that attitude change.

When I was little, my mom used to play hand puppet games. That would definitely cheer me up! I held my hands in front of the mirror and I pretended my left hand was a dog. He said, "Hey, got a biscuit?" And my other hand responded, "No, but I've got a bone."

### *TIME OUT!*

*Ha, ha! That's a good one, right? Okay, so maybe you think it's weird that I tried making jokes about my skeleton curse, but what else was I supposed to do? Cry? Yeah, a lot of good that did me. Sure, maybe other girls would have cried for, like, ever at the thought of turning into a skeleton, but not me. I'm not most girls. Besides, I know you would have made jokes, too. C'mon. I know you're even trying to think of some funny ones right now. But don't bother telling me the joke about the skeleton who wouldn't cross the road because I've heard it, like, a million times. Oh, you don't know that one? Well, he didn't have the GUTS to do it! Get it? Guts . . . skeleton . . . never mind.*

After working on my attitude change for a few hours, I started to feel better. If Mom were here, she'd be proud. Whispering like she was in the room with me, I said, "Hey, Mom, what do you think, maybe some barbeque sauce with my ribs?" I knew if she'd been there she would have laughed. She loved to eat spare ribs.

The jokes and games almost made me feel happy again. Like something about me was okay with the way things were turning out, even if they weren't perfect. Although Mom had done this to me, I knew she had a good reason for it. She loved me too much to do something mean.

I felt like smiling when I went to bed, but without skin, my teeth just clinked together. I was so happy I drifted off to sleep easily. In my dreams, my mom stood at her grave. "Ciiiiiiin-dyyyyy," she said in that same singsong voice. "You haven't viiiiii-sited me yet." She motioned to me, then floated behind her headstone and disappeared.

Morning came too soon. I wished I could have dreamt of Mom forever. *Mom!* I dressed, raced downstairs, ignored the need for breakfast, and grabbed my coat. "I'm going to the cemetery," I said to Dad who sat on the couch watching the news.

He turned off the television and got up. "I don't think that's such a good idea."

I shrugged. "I'm going anyway."

"Then I'm coming with you." Dad grabbed his jacket from the closet.

I sighed. "I'm nearly twelve, so I think I can handle it. Besides, nothing's going to happen." Well, maybe I'd be tied to the ground by skeleton vines again, but it was a chance I had to take.

Dad gave me one of his looks. It said, *Yesterday you were flailing on top of your Mom's grave. Maybe counseling is a better idea than visiting the cemetery again.*

"Trust me." I took Dad's hand and squeezed.

"Oh, all right," he sighed. "But if you're not back in thirty minutes . . ."

"No need to call the National Guard. I'll be fine. And I'll see you in an hour."

"Fine." He tapped his watch. "One hour."

When I arrived at Mom's grave, Ms. Wanda stood there holding a bunch of yellow roses. "Hello, sugah. Come to see your momma?"

"Um, yeah."

"Well, that's nice. I'm sure she loves your visits."

"Yeah," I said wishing my mom could know that I'd visited her before. But she couldn't know that. She was dead.

Yet, she kept calling me. Or maybe that was just me and my overactive, wishful-thinking imagination.

"Tell me something, sugah. You visited her at night yet?"

My heart leapt into my throat. "At night?" Cemeteries were creepy enough during the day. There was no way anyone would get me beyond the iron gates after dark. Especially after what had happened with the vines.

"Of course. Isn't that when magic comes to life?"

"M-m-magic?" I said. How could Ms. Wanda know about magic? It was the second time she'd mentioned it, too. My body shivered. She was really starting to freak me out.

"You do still believe in magic, don't you, sugah?"

### TIME OUT!

*Every story needs an old lady to help make the plot interesting, right? Snow White had the old lady witch. The Little Mermaid had the sea witch. Sleeping Beauty had the sorceress. Oh, wait. Those women tried to kill the main characters. Plus, they were witches. In that case, super-nice-old-lady-from-next-door must just be wacky in the head. Right? RIGHT?*

"Like the magic of Christmas? Or the magic of childhood?" I gulped.

"That's one way of looking at it." She smiled her sweet Southern smile, showing her pearly whites. "But I was thinking more like *magic*." She waved her hand in a sweeping

motion over the grave. White vines started to grow around my feet.

Not the vines! Last time I'd seen them they tried to pull me into the ground. I let out a scream. "I do believe in spooks—I mean magic. I do believe in magic. I do, I do, I do."

"You all right, sugah?" Ms. Wanda extended her hand. Except it was all bone. There was no skin. Her hand was a boney, white skeleton. A boney, white skeleton hand holding a bouquet of roses.

"AAAHH!" I shrieked, closing my eyes tight. My brain screamed, *Run!* But my body said, *I can't!*

Ms. Wanda grabbed my wrist. Her boney fingers cutting into my skin. "You all right, child?"

I pulled back, trying to yank away. She wasn't going to take me with her.

"Cindy," she snapped. "Open your eyes, sugah."

My eyelids fluttered open. I glanced at Ms. Wanda's hand gripped around my wrist. No skeleton hand. I looked at my feet. No vines. "What the . . . ?" I said, my voice trembling.

She inched closer, putting a hand to my forehead, but I squirmed away. "You got a fever?"

I shook my head. No fever. Just a skeleton curse. And a very bad case of the heebie jeebies.

"This sho' has been tough on you, ain't it? You think you gonna be okay?"

I stared at her, my eyes feeling like they might pop out of my head. Ms. Wanda was a witch. A freaky, scary witch. She had to be. If she was an evil witch, did that make my mom bad, too? In that case, were all witches bad? Would I ever be able to trust anyone?

I nodded. "Yeah, uh-huh, sure." But I wasn't about to stick around for more freaky stuff to happen—or to find out what she'd do to me—so I raced home as fast as I could.

Why did I ever have to go to the cemetery? If I'd just stayed home, everything would be fine. Every single time I'd gone there I'd seen white vines that turned into skeleton hands. Maybe I was going crazy, just like Dad probably thought. I bet it was the curse that turned me into a raving lunatic—or Ms. Wanda Fey, with her freaky skeleton vines that made me nutso.

I slammed the door behind me, collapsing against it.

"That was quick," Dad said after the door closed.

My throat was dry as a cracker, making it impossible to swallow. "Yep," I said, breathless, my face feeling as white as a ghost, my stomach aching like I would get sick any second. I tossed my coat on the bench near the door. "The gate was locked." He didn't need to know I was seeing things—and probably going crazy—and that I was so totally freaked out I would probably never go back to the cemetery ever again.

# chapter 6

Maybe Ms. Wanda was a witch and so was my mom, but none of that really mattered. I had to figure out how to live with this curse.

When night came, I jumped out of bed and raced to the mirror. Standing there, studying my skeleton frame, I tapped a boney finger against my chin. I noticed I could see all of my teeth. I turned my head to the side. There were even teeth I couldn't see when I had my skin! Probably because they were the ones buried beneath my gum line just waiting to make me miserable when they popped through. Twelve-year-old molars, I think. Maybe wisdom teeth. I didn't know which.

I rubbed my head. My skull was round and smooth, and to me it seemed perfectly shaped. There was a baby I saw once whose head was shaped like a cone. I thought it was freaky. Good thing my head wasn't like that baby's. Thankfully, my head was perfect, even if it was hairless and skinless.

Then I held my arms out to the side and I realized why my math teacher called me Skinny Minnie. My arms were really thin—well, actually the bones were. In fact, I thought I looked pretty frail. My mom would always say to me when we'd see a heavy person, "They're not fat. Just big boned." Well, I was definitely *not* big boned. Even when I had my skin on, sometimes the other kids teased me, telling me I had chicken legs.

A thought came to my mind. There was something I remembered from Vicki Larson's science project—feet have lots of bones. I decided to put that theory to the test. I sat down on my floor, pulled off my socks, wriggled my toes, and started counting.

One, two, three . . . fourteen, fifteen, sixteen . . .

A loud crash sounded down the street. I jumped, distracted from my counting, and raced to the window in time to hear the loudest, fiercest howl I've ever laid ears on. I scanned up and down the street but there wasn't anything in sight. Not even a single dog. Which was definitely strange for my block—there were almost more dogs than people.

Dad came running into my room. "Was that you? Are you howling?"

"Ahh!" I shrieked, grabbing for a blanket to hide behind. "Don't you knock?"

"Sorry—" he gasped as he saw my skeleton body. He looked like he might puke as he slowly backed away. "I . . . I . . . just—"

"Whatever." I turned my back to him, ashamed that he

couldn't love me as a skeleton, especially when I was working so hard to accept myself.

The door clicked shut and I knew he was gone.

I shrugged and sat back down on the carpet in the middle of my room. I had to get my mind off him.

One, two, three . . . twenty-four, twenty-five, twenty-six. *Ha! It's true!* Vicki Larson was right! She really was good for something other than stealing Ethan.

Since my hands looked like they had tons of bones, I thought I'd count those, too. Sure enough, there were twenty-seven.

As I stood up, I saw my reflection flash in the mirror. That was when I noticed the weirdest part—I didn't have a belly and I could see all the way through my body! I stuck my hand under my ribcage, reached straight back, and touched my spine. *Cool.* Maybe at some point, it would have its advantages. Like if I had to battle a ninja, I'd be really flexible—they'd be swinging their swords and all I'd have to do is reach back and touch my spine. They'd probably freak out and go running the other way. If anyone were around to see it, they'd call me a hero.

That thought made me feel tired—or maybe it was just that I had been standing in front of a mirror for hours and hours, making expressionless faces and counting bones—so I climbed back into bed.

I dreamt I lay in a field of flowers. But I didn't dream of skeletons, vines, or my mom.

If it hadn't been for the eerie silence, I probably would have slept all day. But when the sunlight poured in my room, I sat up and rubbed my heavy eyes, put on my robe, and went downstairs. Dad had left a note on the kitchen counter. It said,

*Had to run an errand. Be back soon. Waffles are in the toaster oven. Syrup is in the pantry. Please drink milk. It's good for your bones.*

There was a smiley face after that, like he thought I wouldn't get the joke or something.

The waffles were still warm and I soaked them in syrup. I even poured myself that glass of milk Dad suggested. I took my breakfast into the family room, turned on the television, and watched cartoons. To my surprise, they were actually funny, and I thought maybe something about me felt better, happier. Like maybe not so sad about my mom being gone. But that thought made me sad again because I realized just how much I still missed her.

When I finished eating, I put my dishes in the sink. That was the same moment Dad came home.

"Good morning, Lovie." He patted my head. "How was breakfast?"

"Good," I said. "Thanks."

"Would you like to go out today?"

"And do what?" I twisted a golden lock of hair around my finger. After studying my hairless head all night, it almost felt weird to touch something that wasn't bone.

"How about shopping? Girls like shopping, right?"

"Yes." I sighed. I couldn't believe he had to ask me that. I was almost twelve. What twelve-year-old girl didn't like shopping? "Yes, Dad. Girls like shopping."

"How about some new clothes? Girls like clothes, don't they?"

"Yes, Dad. Girls like clothes."

"Well, then. We're going out to get you some clothes."

"Sounds great," I said completely unenthusiastically. I didn't want to get super excited because although I had gone shopping with my dad in the past, Mom was always with us. Shopping with him alone was another story.

"And then we'll go for lunch," he said, like it was an added bonus. "You like burgers, right?"

This time I didn't answer him, I just gave him a look. It said, *If I have to tell you "yes" one more time, I'm not going with you.*

"Of course you like burgers. Who doesn't like burgers?" Dad gave a small, awkward laugh.

It wasn't until he reached the word "burgers" for the second time, that I noticed he was twitchy and nervous. Dad was definitely out of character . . . or hiding something. But I knew better than to ask, so I just kept a close eye on him. It could have been that his only daughter was a skeleton, but I had a sneaking suspicion it was something else.

## chapter 7

Even though I thought Dad was trying to pull a fast one on me with all the shopping and burger eating, he didn't. We just went out and had a good time. He even knew enough to leave the store while I tried on clothes. It didn't matter that he was gone almost an hour before he came back because it gave me more time to browse.

Part of me wondered if he was just trying really hard to accept me. Maybe he thought that if he loved me enough during the day—and tried really hard to make me happy—it would change how he felt at night, like he might not feel so weird around me. Or maybe he just thought all his niceness made up for not comforting me when I was a skeleton.

After dinner and the sun had set, alone in my room, I slumped on my bed realizing how different I was. Not a bad different. There were just changes I'd noticed. Like, I didn't need to sleep as much as I usually did. That's probably why I kept waking at night. Either that or I was getting used to being awake so I could give myself those mini-pep talks and play bone counting games. Whatever it was, I kind of liked being a night owl.

There was also the fact that I couldn't feel hot or cold. Which made me think that maybe I couldn't feel pain either. I'd have to figure that out sooner or later and tonight was as good a time as any. I'd have to be careful, though, because I'd heard broken bones hurt and I didn't want to have to deal with that.

I needed some motivation. *Music.* That's it! I raced over to my radio and turned it on. "Bad to the Bone" blasted through my room as I danced around, strumming my air guitar.

Since dancing didn't hurt, I decided to take more drastic measures. Charging full force, I ran into a wall. It was definitely not one of my smarter ideas. It hurt. A lot. Lesson learned.

Cindy–0, Pain–1.

End game.

### TIME OUT!

*Hey. I can hear you, y'know. My pain is no laughing matter. Okay, so I'll admit it was a little funny. Fine, it was actually a lot funny. Remember that time you called your teacher "Mom?" Well it was almost as funny as that. But not quite.*

Anything had to be better than running into walls.

My soft bed! That would definitely be much more fun. I climbed on and jumped as high as I could. When I landed there was a loud noise. Hoping it wasn't a burglar trying to break in the house or something, I got real still and quiet, listening.

But the sound was gone. Convinced I was just hearing things, I leapt into the air. I came down fast, bouncing on the springy mattress, with a clinking, clunking sound. I froze. Moved an elbow. *Clunk!*

The noise came from me!

Who knew that being a skeleton was so noisy? All that stuff in science class about tendons, muscles, and skin was probably pretty important. I guess I should have paid better attention. Then I would have known that bone against bone made a whole lot of clamor. I was like my very own science lesson! Talk about hands-on learning.

I walked around my room like a soldier. When I lifted my leg, it made a noise. It went, *crack, crack, click.*

With my arms in the air, I jumped up and did my biggest and best jumping jack ever. My bones went *ting, ting, ting, ting* and *clunk, clunk, clunk.* It reminded me of all those old black and white World War Two movies with air-raid attacks.

All those noises made me think of drums . . . my rib cage did look an awful lot like a xylophone. There was a hairbrush on the sink in my bathroom. A perfect mallet! I grabbed it and tapped each rib. The smaller ones made high notes and the bigger ones made low notes. I was like my own one-man band! I tried to play a song we had learned in music class, but I couldn't get it quite right. When I ran the brush up and down my ribcage, it made a *b-dah rump, b-dah rump* sound. It tickled so bad, I hunched over and laughed.

Through my fit of laughter, I noticed the bathtub which, for some reason, made me think about swimming. Since the temperature didn't matter, I turned on both the hot and cold water. It rushed from the faucet, filling the tub to the top. I climbed in, water slopping over the edge of the tub.

There wasn't enough room to swim, but I kicked my feet and swished my hands at my side.

That's when my world became silent, like someone had muffled all the sound. No creaking, cracking, clicking, ting-ing, or clunking. Just swishing. It made me feel peaceful.

And sleepy.

I climbed out of the tub, dried off, slipped on fleece paja-mas, and climbed into bed. Cozy and comfortable, sleep came easily. I dreamt of skeletons dancing in my room. Except these skeletons didn't clatter when they moved. They were quiet as could be. I wanted to be able to move soundlessly like they did. Even though I still made lots of noise dancing in my dream and even though the other skel-etons laughed, it didn't make me feel bad. I just laughed too.

"You were quite rowdy last night," Dad said, not looking up from his newspaper. He took a sip of coffee from the mug in his other hand.

"Sorry," I said, glad his face was buried because I didn't want him to give me a "look."

"What were you doing?"

There was one word that parents never understood, but didn't need an explanation for. "Playing," I said as I sat at the table beside him.

## TIME OUT!

*What is it about parents anyway? Weren't they kids once? Did they forget how much fun it is to play? Okay, so maybe at almost-twelve, I'm too old to play with toys, but it sure amused me to dance around and play my bones like music. I bet you would have done the same thing. Just like I know you were making skeleton jokes. Just like I know that tonight when you go to bed you're going to try dancing and see if your bones make noise. Don't bother. It doesn't work. You have to be a skeleton.*

Dad put his paper down and gave me a look. Yep—there it was. The very thing I hoped to avoid. The look said, *Aren't you a little old to be playing?* Then, before I could give him a look in return, he got up and put some bread in the toaster. When it popped up, my dad grabbed it. He quickly dropped the toast on a plate and shook his hand at his side.

"So, Cindy," he said, nursing his burnt finger. "I was thinking."

Because I didn't want to seem too interested, I faked a yawn. "Yeah, about what?"

"About your curse." He handed me the toast, complete with cinnamon sugar on top.

"My curse?" Was he really willing to talk about it? I looked at him oddly. Dad looked at me oddly. "Oh right. What about it?" I picked at the bread, trying to hide the fact that even though at first I hated every minute of being a skeleton, I kind of enjoyed it now. Well, not exactly *enjoyed,* but tolerated, I suppose.

Dad refilled his drink and sat across from me, wrapping his hands around a steamy mug of coffee. He leaned back, trying to be casual, but I could tell he was actually twitchy because his pinky finger trembled. "I think I might be able to get you some help."

chapter 8

My eyes darted from the sparkly cinnamon sugar to my dad's face. What made him think I needed help? More importantly, why didn't he know that I didn't *want* help? My mouth dropped open in defense, but I snapped it closed and tightened my jaw so he couldn't see my shock. Unable to stop the tremble in my own hands, I dropped the toast on the table.

"Help?" I gulped.

"Yeah, help." Dad tried to smile confidently, but his quick, uneven breaths gave away his insecurity. "So you don't have to be ..."

"A skeleton." The food in my mouth tasted bitter. "It's okay to say it, Dad. A skeleton."

He dropped his gaze to his cup of coffee, refusing to look at me.

With a sigh, I crossed my arms and sat back. "Yeah, I didn't think you could."

I couldn't finish my breakfast. My stomach felt too sick. Even though Dad didn't make me go to my room, I threw my chair back and marched there anyway. He'd never love me the way I was. In fact, he couldn't stand that I was freaky-cursed-skeleton-girl. I think he really only loved me when I was normal middle-school-girl Cindy. Maybe that's why he was so twitchy and nervous the other day. He'd been sneaking around trying to find answers when I was busy trying on clothes!

I sat in my room all day—completely avoiding my dad. He didn't bother to check on me or bring me any food, either. When dusk came I filled the tub with water and bubbles. If it didn't help me relax, at least it would give me something to do.

As the tub filled, the phone rang.

"It's Sarah!" Dad shouted from downstairs.

I ran so fast, I nearly tripped. Grabbing the phone from my dresser, I said, "Chicky Monkey!" before it even touched my ear.

"Chickeroo." Her voice was ten octaves higher than normal. Obviously she was happy to be back.

Dad breathed heavily on the other end of the phone. "Hang up, Dad! I got it!" The phone clicked. "Okay, he's gone. Tell me about your trip." My head tingled with a spark of excitement.

"Can I come over?"

"Sure," I said. But then I remembered it would be skeleton-time soon. "I mean, no. Not today."

"Um. Okay," she said. "Maybe tomorrow? Then we can do a sleepover."

"Sure. Maybe tomorrow." But deep inside my gut, I knew I wouldn't be seeing my best friend for a long time. Not at a sleepover, anyway. Because there was no way I'd share my secret skeleton curse thing—not even with Sarah.

### TIME OUT!

*Sure, she's my BFF (my chicky monkey), but how could I possibly tell her, "Hey Sarah, just thought you'd like to know that right before my mom died she cursed me and now I turn into a skeleton every night, so don't freak out or anything." Yeah, that would go over big. She's cool—but no one would ever accept a skeleton-girl for a friend. ☹*

"So I'll talk to you later then, right?"

"Sure thing. I'll call you," I said, knowing I wouldn't really call her. Not until I figured out this skeleton-thing anyway.

Things would be very different for me. No more sleepovers, no shopping or going to movies after dark. It wasn't fair.

I slipped into the tub and sulked in the bath. My skin didn't have a chance to turn pruny and wrinkly because I transformed into a skeleton while I sat in the lukewarm water. Just like last time, there was no creaking, clacking, clinging, or clunking. Just swishing.

When I finished feeling sorry for myself, I put on a robe,

grabbed a magazine, and plopped on my favorite beanbag chair.

There was a picture of some kids dressed in Halloween costumes. It must have been an old issue, because Halloween was long over. I laughed at the thought that I wouldn't need a costume this year. I already had one.

That gave me an idea!

When it was completely dark, and I was sure my dad was asleep, I snuck past his room—remembering to be as quiet as possible because my bones made an awful lot of racket. Then I tiptoed downstairs, carefully opened the front door, and went outside.

Other than a few houses with their front lights on, the street was still pretty dark. The moon was just a little crescent-like sliver and I suddenly couldn't remember the last time I had seen it.

Since it was so late, I figured everyone on the block was probably fast asleep, so I wasn't sure how this would all work out. But that wasn't going to stop me from pulling off the prank of the century. In fact, it made it even better.

When I spied a blue house with black shutters—Mr. Peterkin's place—I knew it was the perfect choice because he worked late at night. I remembered seeing him sometimes, sitting in the front room, typing away on a keyboard.

I also remembered how cranky he was.

Mr. Peterkin always yelled at kids who walked across his yard. He also sprayed the garden hose at dogs that got too close to his lawn.

Two years ago he dismantled my scooter when he found it in his driveway. And last year he ran over my bike, even though it wasn't in his driveway. Although he hadn't done anything this year, I was sure he would.

As if that didn't make him unbearable enough as a neighbor, he was strange, too. He grew large pumpkins in his backyard greenhouse year round. Rumor had it that he made his wife bake him pumpkin treats every day. Pumpkin cookies, pumpkin bars, pumpkin bread, pumpkin rolls, pumpkin muffins, and pumpkin pie. If you ask me, it didn't matter how much sugar you added, pumpkin was still a vegetable and there was no way it would ever taste good. Maybe that's what was wrong with Mr. Peterkin—all the vegetables had gone to his head.

It didn't make sense that Mrs. Peterkin could be married to such a cranky old man because she was just as nice as . . . pie! But not pumpkin pie. Maybe a sweet apple pie with loads of cinnamon and sugar. Anyway, I hoped she was asleep.

I crept to their window. Maybe Mr. Peterkin was working. But when I peeked in, I saw that he wasn't. He was laid back in his recliner chair facing the big picture window. Glasses sat at the tip of his nose. One hand seemed to rest mid-air, as he flipped channels with the remote.

There was a spot on the ground below the window just perfect for my prank. I knelt there a moment, then reached up and knocked on the glass. Mr. Peterkin sat up quickly, his chair making a screeching sound. He stood up. But he never walked toward the window. After what seemed like endless silence, the chair squeaked as he sat back down. I figured it was the chair pleading for him to get up.

I kept trying to imagine the look Mr. Peterkin would have on his face when he saw a skeleton outside his window. The whole thing just seemed really funny to me and I giggled uncontrollably.

Laughter from my not-really-there belly made me shake all over. My hand trembling, I reached up and knocked at the window a second time. The chair moaned again, followed by the sound of footsteps. Heavy, fast footsteps.

Since I didn't dare peek inside, I could only listen. The footsteps grew louder and louder until they suddenly stopped and I wondered if he'd gone to the kitchen for a pumpkin treat. Then I saw his breath fogging up the glass. It was the perfect time to make my move. The excitement built inside me so much that I couldn't contain it another second. I jumped up. I shook my hands above my head and swayed in place. My bones rattled. Then I made a ghostly noise, trying to be as scary as possible.

My voice went, "Oooohhh, oooooo, aaaahhhh."

Mr. Peterkin took one look at me and let out this moaning yell, "Uggghhh! Eh, oh, oh." Then he did this move where he tried really hard to run away. But his legs just ran in place, not going anywhere. It was like his feet were on marbles and he just slipped in the same spot—kind of like a cartoon, his legs spinning in a gigantic circle. Eventually he got enough momentum that those feet running in place finally moved.

But they propelled him backward instead of forward. He tripped over the coffee table and landed on the sofa. Almost like he'd intended to sit back down, except the expression on his face told me differently.

### TIME OUT!

*Ohmygosh! Did you just spurt milk through your nose? *Snort* You have to teach me that trick because it's the funniest thing I've ever seen. But you might want to wipe it up before . . . never mind. Looks like it's already dripping down your shirt.*

Thrilled with my victory (which might have been just a tad vengeful, but not at all overrated), I jumped up and down wishing I had someone to high five, but realized this celebration was all mine.

Inside, Mr. Peterkin didn't move from the sofa and his expression was still the same—his eyes huge and his face pale, mouth open wide. Kind of like when my Dad saw me for the first time. Mr. Peterkin clutched at his chest, gasping for air.

Unable to control my laughter, I fell in the grass and rolled around. I slapped my hand on the ground and kicked my feet. My body ached from laughing so hard.

The laughter was really loud. So loud that I started thinking Mr. Peterkin might come outside to see who made so much noise. If he did that, he'd see me sprawled out on the grass and maybe this time he wouldn't be scared. Instead, I bet he'd be really angry because he loves his lawn. If he was angry enough, I'd probably get really nervous and say something stupid. If that happened, he was sure to figure out that it was I who scared him and then I'd be in big trouble.

I figured I ought to hide. Going home wasn't an option because if Mr. Peterkin was watching, he'd see me go in my house. That wouldn't be such a great idea. I'm like one thousand percent positive he'd call my dad and warn him about the skeleton on the loose. Since my dad is pretty smart, he'd figure out what I'd been up to.

There was a set of bushes between Mrs. Mellon's and Ms. Wanda's houses: the perfect hiding spot. Although I'd have to wait there until I saw all the lights go out in Mr. Peterkin's house, it was better than the alternative of getting caught.

With my best ninja-style stealth, I snuck over to the bushes and hid. There was a loud howl—it was the same noise as the other night. I peeked out between the branches and hoped that the dog was far away. I mean, what dog didn't like bones? I'd be a perfect midnight snack. Thankfully, there wasn't a single dog in sight. So I ducked behind the bushes again and continued to wait.

I waited.

And waited.

Turned out, Mr. Peterkin could stay up really late.

Or . . .

Maybe I gave the old man a heart attack. Maybe I needed to call an ambulance . . .

Thankfully, just as I was about to dash over the bushes to

Mr. Peterkin's house, the lights went out in his living room and I knew he was just fine. Relieved that I didn't literally scare him to death, I turned to go home. Two steps later, my foot caught on a tree root and I tripped. When I stood up I was eye to eye with the biggest, hairiest dog I'd ever seen.

chapter 9

*Run!* my brain screamed. My body listened and I took off running. As. Fast. As. I. Could. Thoughts buzzed through my head. The only one I really heard was, *That dog is going to eat me!*

I needed to get somewhere safe. Somewhere that a dog couldn't go. Somewhere that kept dogs out and people safely in. But I couldn't think of anything.

My feet ached but I kept running because the dog's panting was right on my tail! I booked it past all the houses, past the park, and straight to the gates of the cemetery.

*Think.* I glanced at the fence. It shined with black ice glowing in the moonlight. I touched the wrought iron. *Think.* My eyes scanned along the fence. The cemetery looked even scarier than it was in the daylight. Way scarier than any movie I'd ever watched with my mom.

But it was surrounded on all sides with fencing. "Something to keep dogs out," I whispered. I'd be safe in the cemetery. Right?

### TIME OUT!

*I know. It's late. It's dark. It's like a horror movie and I'm like that stupid girl that always gets caught by the crazy man who kills everyone. Go ahead. Scream. Tell me not to go. Chances are though, you'll just get frustrated. 'Cause that stupid girl always opens the door to the basement. She always goes down into the dark. She always gets . . . gulp . . . well, you know the rest. Dumb girl. And tonight, I'm that stupid, stupid girl.*

The dog growled and panted behind me. *Must climb the fence,* I thought. I scrambled all the way to the top, then jumped over and landed hard, my bones clattering. Then I turned to the dog, put my hand on my hip and said, "Sorry, Rover, these bones aren't on the menu." The dog put his snout in the air and howled.

I was safe.

Or was I? After all, I was in a creepy cemetery, all alone, after dark.

I was so nervous my teeth chattered.

Maybe this wasn't the best place for me to be. What if someone saw me? They might try to bury my bones in a grave and I was too young to be buried alive even if I was a skeleton.

As I walked through the cemetery my bones clunked and clinked. There was nothing I could do to quiet the noise, so I trudged onward until I found Mom's white headstone. At the very least, I'd feel safe near her for the night.

Or maybe I wouldn't. After all, I'd seen white vines at her grave. They tried to pull me into the ground. But Ms. Wanda had been there all those times, hadn't she? She was nowhere to be seen, so maybe I'd be okay.

Too exhausted to care, I collapsed on my mom's grave.

A rustling noise came from behind her headstone. "M-m-mom," I said, thinking of skeleton vines. My stutter had to be from the cold because I wasn't afraid. Well, okay, maybe I was a little scared. Fine. I was a lot scared.

When I searched around me, thankfully, there was nothing. No white vines. No skeletons hands. Well, except my own. So I leaned on the headstone and rubbed its surface with my fingers.

"I miss you, Mom." If I had been normal-Cindy, I would have cried. But being a skeleton, there were no tears. "I wish I could see you again."

"Well, sugah, I do think that's a real good poss-i-bil-i-ty."

"Wh-who's there?" I shot upright, my body trembling.

"It's me, sugah. It's Ms. Wanda." She stepped forward, her skin and clothes so dark she blended in with the night.

*No, no, no!* Not Ms. Wanda the freaky witch! "W-w-what?" I said.

"A visit." She smiled. "I do believe it's long overdue."

"B-b-but, she's dead."

"She sure is, sugah." She stalked toward me. "And you sure is stubborn. Ain't nobody told you that before? Stubborn and thickheaded."

"But I don't want to die." My body shook. I didn't want this crazy lady to kill me.

Ms. Wanda lifted both of her hands in the air. I covered my eyes hoping it would be over quickly. "Cindy—sugah—don't be afraid. It won't hurt one bit."

"It w-w-won't?"

"Of course not." She laughed. "You already a skeleton, ain't you?"

"Uh, uh, okay. Yeah." I knew I could still feel pain as a skeleton, so I knew she was lying. Dying was going to hurt. I straightened up tall, but hid my face behind my hands.

Ms. Wanda let out a sigh. "I'm not gonna kill you."

I peeked between my fingers. "You're not?"

"Course not. What good would that do you? Certainly wouldn't help me none, either."

I would have blinked my eyes, but they only rolled around in my head. "Well, how can I see her if she's dead?"

"That's why you're a skeleton, sugah. And that's why I'm here." Ms. Wanda beamed, her white teeth lighting up the night. "I'm gonna give that last little touch o' magic."

"Magic?" My bones trembled. "You mean like Mom?"

Ms. Wanda nodded.

"So you're not a freaky witch?"

Ms. Wanda laughed so hard, she bent in half, slapping her knee with a hand.

"So . . . are you like a fairy godmother?"

She smiled. A great, big, sparkling, white-toothed smile. I couldn't believe it. I had my very own fairy godmother!

All of a sudden, it dawned on me. "You're not going to sing, are you?"

She laughed. "Heavens, no! There's no bippity-boppity-boo with me."

## TIME OUT!

*You're thanking me right now, aren't you? No song and dance. No music with a chubby old lady singing a song with made-up words and changing pumpkins into a coach and mice into horses. It's okay. You don't even have to say thank you. Just keep reading, and I promise no one will break out into song. Unless of course you want that, then I'd be happy to arrange it.*

Ms. Wanda pulled a long wand from her coat sleeve then waved her hand over the grave. "And now . . . to fulfill that promise I made to your momma."

As she waved her wand-filled hand over the grave, something popped into my brain, and I wondered why I'd never noticed before. Wanda = wand . . . and fairies carry wands. Fey = fairy . . . and fairies can be godmothers. Wanda Fey = Fairy Godmother. How come it took me so long to figure that out? She was right—I really was stubborn and thickheaded.

Suddenly, the ground below me rattled.

It shook. And quaked.

I leapt to my feet but I couldn't run. My brain screamed, *Goooooo now!* But my body said, *I can't.*

A crack formed in the ground around the grave. The same white vines I'd seen before crept toward me inching closer and closer. I wanted to run, but Ms. Wanda held out her arm and pointed at the grave. The vines had become skeleton hands again. But instead of lunging at me, they were . . . waving hello?

I rubbed my eyes.

Yep.

They were definitely waving.

Shyly, I waved back. Then the earth quaked again and a rectangular hole, no larger than a shoebox, opened at the base of the headstone. The viny skeleton hands formed into a ball and rolled around the grave.

"M-m-mom."

Ms. Wanda put her hand on my shoulder—something my dad could never do when I was a skeleton.

"No," a voice said.

"Great." I looked at my fairy godmother for reassurance. "Now I'm hearing voices?"

Ms. Wanda laughed heartily.

"You sure are," the voice said. "Mine." A little white mouse shot out from behind the grave and ran across my toes. A skeleton mouse. "I'm your friendly Underworld tour guide," he said.

"Underworld?"

"Yes. It's *under* your world."

I tried to chuckle, but it came out all nervous, kind of like a grunt.

"The name's Cheddar." He put out his hand as if to shake it. "Don't confuse it with Chester. Got it?"

I took his tiny skeleton hand in mine and shook it.

"And remember, it's Cheddar, C-H-E-D-D-A-R."

"Like the cheese?"

"Why does everyone ask that?" he said grumpily. "Now c'mon. We haven't got all night." He shook his little fist. "And watch where you walk—I hate being stepped on. Do you know how difficult it is to reassemble these bones?"

"Wouldn't that be painful?" I didn't want to hurt him, that's for sure. "I thought broken bones hurt."

"Sure it does, kid. For the Living. But I'm dead. Big difference." The mouse jumped into the hole in the ground and disappeared.

Ms. Wanda patted my shoulder. "Go on, sugah. She's been waiting for you."

I nodded, trying to swallow my fear.

Just as I was about to step into the hole, a bubble gum pink elevator shot out of the ground, sending me flying backward. My bones rattled when I landed.

A glass door surrounded by flashing white lights opened and carnival music flooded into the night. The letters R.I.P. were engraved into the pink metal sides.

"Rip?" I said aloud. "Like Rest In Peace?"

The mouse leapt off the top of the elevator and landed on my skull. He crawled down my spine to my shoulder, then pulled on my jawbone, like he was going to whisper in my ear. "No, no, no. You've got it all wrong." He sounded really irritated. I could tell by the way his bones rattled and shook when he talked.

I covered my mouth and giggled at the cranky little mouse. "So what does it mean?"

Even though he was a skeleton and he couldn't give me a look, I imagined one anyway. It said, *You annoying little girl. Just do what you're told and stop asking questions.*

Cheddar jumped to the ground. "Real Incorpsified Paradise," he said. "Where the dead are just a mummy away." He made a gesture with his hands in the air, like there was an invisible sign floating above him. "That's our slogan."

"Dead. Mummy. That's funny." My body shook with nervous laughter. "Oh, wait." I got real serious. "Does that mean I'll see dead bodies?" If I had skin I would have snarled my lips at him. "Gross."

The mouse let out a long sigh. "You coming or not?" he said as he twitched his tail.

I looked around, feeling a twang of apprehension build in my bones. I was about to leave the only world I'd ever known. But it seemed worth it because I really wanted to see my mom. Then I started thinking . . . what if I didn't like it there? What if something horrible waited for me in the Underworld? What if I had to see dead people all the time? That might be gross. Especially if they were bloody and full of maggots. Maybe I'd be freaked out by all that death. But a bigger question settled in my chest, like a heavy brick weighing me down. Was I really ready to leave my dad, my BFF Sarah, and my biggest crush, Ethan?

I swallowed hard. If I wanted to see my mom, then I had no other choice. So with a great, big, brave breath—my decision made, at all costs—I stepped inside the elevator.

chapter 10

"Have a good time, dear." Ms. Wanda waved.

The elevator dropped into the earth so fast that I flew into the ceiling. My body stuck there like I was being sucked into place with a giant vacuum. Since I was skeleton-Cindy, my bones rattled, a lot. If I'd been normal-Cindy, my guts would be in my skull and my brains would have flown out my ears. *Smart thinking, Mom.*

A second later, the doors opened to a sunny world with purple skies and billowy clouds. Turquoise-colored astro-turf stretched as far as I could see. There weren't any of those pesky dandelion weeds that Dad hated pulling all summer long. Plus, he wouldn't have to mow the lawn. He would love it here.

"This is the Underworld?" I looked around, puzzled. "I mean, R.I.P," I said, correcting myself.

"Well, what did you expect? Devils with pitchforks? Fire and brimstone? Darkness and floating spirits?"

### TIME OUT!

*Yep. I kind of did. Didn't you? I mean, he did say it was the Underworld (a.k.a. R.I.P – where the dead are just a mummy away). What else was I supposed to think? Every book I've ever read gave the same description of it. How gloomy. What's wrong with authors nowadays anyway? Maybe they need someone to talk to, like a guidance counselor . . . or maybe they just need to take my mom's advice and get an attitude adjustment. Oh, and by the way, nice shirt you're wearing. It's a good choice. Brings out the color of your eyes.*

Cheddar twitched his tail. "The Living are all the same. Everything is always so depressing. Can't think happy thoughts, can you?"

"Sure I can." I wanted to smile, but without skin, my teeth only clinked together. "I just thought one right now."

"Oh. And what would that be?"

"That I'm not going to step on you."

"Humpf." Cheddar's tail twitched once as he scurried ahead. "C'mon. Hurry up."

I rushed to keep up with him. Skeleton mice were much quicker than I imagined.

Cheddar scampered on, guiding me along a path which led through a flower-filled meadow. Pink daisies danced in the breeze. Butterflies that glowed neon green floated above them. The air smelled of cotton candy, caramel apples, and kettle corn. It was a carnival lover's paradise!

Ahead was a ticket booth. When we reached it, Cheddar crawled up my arm and grunted. "Let me handle this." Then he tapped on the wooden sill.

A man with dark eyes and a Yankees baseball cap twirled a cigar in his mouth. "Haw-m-ny?" He yawned and slumped against the frame. A nametag on the pocket of his shirt identified him as Bert.

"What did he say?" I whispered, hoping the man wouldn't hear me.

Cheddar ignored me and scurried down my arm and onto the counter. "Two, please, Bert."

My chin dropped in shock. "We need tickets?"

"Did you really think we'd get free admission?"

Uh, yeah, I kind of did. "I, ah, I . . ."

Cheddar shook his head. "The Living. Always wanting a handout."

Bert looked at Cheddar, aghast, yanking the cigar from his mouth. "You can't bring the Living in here," he said, his voice escalating and his face reddening.

"The Living? Who said anything about the Living? I was joking. I meant R.D. You know how they are." He pushed a gold coin (which he pulled from between his ribs) across the counter.

I leaned in to Cheddar cupping my hand around my mouth. "What's an R.D.?"

"Recently Deceased." Cheddar's tail twitched nervously.

The man tore off two orange tickets from a large roll and slid them across the counter.

"You'll adjust." Cheddar had a strange tone in his voice that made me uneasy.

Bert smiled suspiciously. There was something about it that made my skin crawl, even though I didn't have any. He was the nicest, creepiest dead guy I'd ever met. "Hv-a-nc-dy," Bert muttered as he shoved the cigar back in his mouth.

"You too." Cheddar took the tickets and tucked them between his ribs. "Shall we?" he said, looking at me, pointing toward a sign that said "R.D.—This Way, Please."

As soon as we were far enough away from Bert, Cheddar let out a sigh of relief. He turned to me and his voice got all serious-like. "The Living aren't allowed in R.I.P., so there are three rules you must abide by."

I started to worry that coming to see my mom in R.I.P. was a mistake. "Okay." I tried not to let my teeth chatter from nerves. "What are they?"

"Well, if you'd give me a chance, I'll tell you. The Living. Always so impatient." Cheddar twitched his tail.

"Sorry."

"Rule number one: Don't talk to strangers."

"Easy enough. My parents have told me that since I was little."

Cheddar tapped his foot.

"Oh, sorry," I said sheepishly. "Okay. What's the next rule?"

"Number two . . ."

I burst into laughter. "You said number two!"

The mouse tipped his head like he didn't understand.

"Number two . . . bathroom humor . . . get it?"

"Humpf. The Living. Always making a joke of something." He twitched his tail. "Are you ready now?"

I nodded. "Uh-hum."

"Good. Rule number two: You're what the locals call an R.D., Recently Deceased, so, if anyone asks, just tell them you're new."

Yeah, I already learned that from Bert. "But I thought you said I shouldn't talk to strangers?"

"For Underkeeper's sake. Would you just let me finish?"

"I'll be good." I crossed a finger over my ribcage where my heart normally would have been. "Promise."

"It's about time." Cheddar crawled up my bones to my shoulder and whispered, "Rule number three is very important."

Ready for the biggest and most super significant announcement ever, I listened closely.

"STAY ON THE PATH!" he yelled.

I jumped back and rubbed the side of my head. "Ow! What did you do that for?"

"Just wanted to make sure you were paying attention. Now follow that yellow brick road."

Cheddar must have been colorblind—or really hungry for some cheese—because the path wasn't yellow. And it wasn't brick. But I didn't say anything because he had such a temper. I didn't laugh either, even if it was a bad attempt at a joke. I figured he'd just get mad at that too.

We walked along a cobblestone path until we reached a fork in the road.

Straight ahead the path led down a road much the same as we'd been on. Pink daisies and other colorful flowers of every variety danced in the breeze. The same neon green butterflies as well as others large enough to be mistaken for birds fluttered in the field. Turquoise meadows of astroturf spread out as far as the eye could see.

A path to my right led toward a carnival, complete with glittering lights, Ferris wheels, and loud music.

But a small, unkempt path on my left was different. Trees without leaves arched across it, their branches reaching, clawing as though they wanted to strangle each other. Strange birds the color of midnight cawed in the trees, flapping their wings angrily at each other. One bird lost a feather. But it didn't float the way most feathers do. It fell with a thud, landing on a small stack of stones. There were other piles of rocks scattered throughout the path, but something else littered the ground. Something that looked like white sticks . . . or maybe they were bones! I didn't want to think about that possibility.

I strained to see farther, but beyond the trees darkness swallowed everything. Pitch black darkness. Moaning sounds floated in the air like weightless spirits. I definitely didn't want to go down that path. Ever. "W-w-what's down that way?" I pointed to the foreboding-looking trail.

Cheddar ignored me, shifting his nose straight ahead, in

the direction of the happier path with flowers. I sighed with relief. While I was curious about the other path, I felt glad to be headed somewhere less scary.

My feet carried us along, down a small hill, until I saw a white picket fence. Inside the fence a little stone cottage with gray-blue shutters invited me with a warm glow. More pink daisies filled the window boxes. It was just like the painting that hung over the fireplace in our house.

I swung the gate open; it made a loud creaking noise. In the open doorway stood a beautiful woman with soft, brown hair pulled into a loose bun. The hem of her floral dress swayed as she dried her hands on the apron tied at her waist.

I couldn't believe my eyes. All I could do was stare at her, my chest aching. "Mom? Is that really you?" She smiled at me and there wasn't a single doubt in my mind. I knew it was her. My legs started running and the rest of me could barely keep up. "Mom! Mom!"

She dashed toward me and we met in the middle of the little cobblestone path. "Cindy!" Mom scooped me into her arms hugging me tight, twirling in a circle. As she squeezed, the smell of her perfume warmed me. It was the best feeling in the whole world. Like all my favorite comfort foods and warm blankets and best dreams all wrapped up in this one happy moment. I'd missed her so much.

Mom put me down, wiping away tears. She smoothed my skull as we studied each other. She was lovelier than I remembered, her face so soft and young like a porcelain doll.

All the worry lines were gone. Even that little *V* between her eyebrows had vanished. It felt good to see her like this—instead of the way she was before she died.

I put my skeleton hand to her rosy cheek. "You look beautiful." If I had been normal-Cindy I would have cried. But, if I'd been normal-Cindy, I also wouldn't have been visiting my mom in R.I.P., either.

"And you're perfect," she said to me.

But I knew I wasn't perfect. I was a skeleton.

"I hoped you wouldn't mind . . ." She gestured at my skeleton body.

I didn't want her to feel bad, plus I was really glad to see her, so it seemed like it didn't matter. "It's worth it," I said.

"That was the only way to get you down here. They don't allow The Living in R.I.P." Mom glanced away, her eyes scanning around the meadow.

Cheddar harrumphed from my shoulder.

Mom cleared her throat, looking quickly at Cheddar. "What am I doing wasting our time? We can discuss all of that later. Now let's get inside."

A fireplace in the far corner lit the room with the glow of a golden fire. There were photos of Dad and me on the walls. I touched a picture of the three of us taken at our one and only trip to the beach.

"Do you remember that?" Mom asked softly.

"Sure do." I might have been little on that vacation, but I remembered every detail as if it were yesterday.

Mom put her hand on my shoulder, almost knocking Cheddar off. He scampered to the other side. "That's the thanks I get?"

"Come on. I have something to show you." Mom led me to an oak door and opened it. Inside was a bedroom with pale blue walls complete with a large bed, a swivel chair, and a star mobile that glistened, casting little sparkles against the walls and ceiling. "Just for you." She smiled.

I clambered in and sat on the bed. "I love it! It's perfect." A basket by the bedside had some magazines in it. Bookshelves surrounded a window overlooking the backyard. On the top shelf were my favorite dolls—including the one I lost when I was little. "How'd you get—"

"It's the magic of R.I.P. Everything you ever loved—or wanted—comes with you. Well, except people."

Mom sat beside me. It felt good to be home. Even if it meant I was a skeleton and not in the real world with living people. I didn't really care.

Out of the corner of my eye I saw something move. The fluffy pillows on the bed squirmed like they were alive. A white paw shot out, stretched, and receded. My bones trembled. The pillow moved again and a skeleton cat emerged. It crawled toward me, purring.

"Scruffy?" It couldn't be! The skeleton cat rubbed his skull against my ribs. "It is you!" I scratched my old cat on top of his skull, right between where his ears would have been.

Cheddar fidgeted on my shoulder. "Cat? Cat. CAT!" He scampered up my spine to my skull. "No one told me there would be a cat."

Mother leaned over and held her palm out for the mouse. He leapt on her hand. "You'll be safe here. Scruffy couldn't reach you if he tried. He's too old and lazy." She placed Cheddar on top of a bookshelf.

"Humpf." Cheddar settled in a spot between my two favorite stuffed dolls, curled up into a tight ball, and went to sleep.

"He'll be quiet for a while." Mom assured as she sat back down next to me on the bed.

I cupped a hand around my mouth so Cheddar couldn't hear. "He sure is grumpy."

"I'm sorry. He's the best I could come up with on short notice. I thought about sending a horse. Sadly, they're expensive and once they've reached R.I.P they don't want to do a lick of work."

"Guess they really didn't like all their work in the real world. I'd probably get tired of someone riding my back all day too."

Mom covered her mouth as she chuckled. "Oh, how I've missed you, my little Cinderella." She hugged me. It was the best feeling in the whole world. Like comfort and warmth. And happiness.

"I missed you, too." Lying back on the pillows, I crossed my arms behind my head, relaxing. I could get used to this. I crossed a foot over my knee.

Mom lay beside me, her soft breath on my face. "How was Dad when you left?"

Dad? Oh, no! I hadn't thought about Dad! I got this achy feeling where my stomach should have been. I was in R.I.P. and would be here forever. I just left Dad at home all by himself. A sob built in my chest; I wanted to cry. I couldn't believe what I'd done. "I never said goodbye to him."

## chapter 11

"Oh, don't you worry about that." Mom snuggled closer. "He'll see you in the morning."

I sat up so fast I felt dizzy. "What do you mean?" This weird feeling flooded through me kind of like when the bathtub makes a mini whirlpool as all the water gets sucked down the drain. "Is Dad going to . . . die?"

"No, silly." Mom rubbed my skull. "You have to go home."

My mouth dropped open. "You mean I'm not staying here?"

Mom got a real serious look on her face. A wrinkle formed on her forehead and her lips pursed into a bow. She shook her head.

"B-b-but . . . I thought I was staying forever." One night was too short to spend with my mom. I needed more time.

"I want you here forever. Believe me." Mom held a breath for a long time and I knew she worked hard not to get emotional. "But if you don't get back to the real world before dawn, you'll remain a skeleton forever."

"I don't care. I'll be a skeleton forever. Just let me stay with you. Please." I started crying, really hard. So hard it bordered on a two-year-old-like tantrum. I just didn't stomp my feet.

## TIME OUT!

*I bet you've done the same thing. It goes like this: First your voice gets kind of whiny. Then you pout your lips. And make puppy dog eyes (although that's normally reserved for when you have to beg for a new pair of jeans or to go out with friends, it works well in most any situation). When that doesn't work, you resort to arm-crossing and a HUFF. Then, if that doesn't give you enough of a reaction, you either start the waterworks or stomping your feet. Am I right? Works like a charm. Every. Time.*

"Cindy, honey, that's just not possible. You can't stay forever."

"Then you can come back with me!"

"But I'm dead. I can't go back." Mom got this distant look on her face and I kind of wondered how much she missed the real world. Did she miss Dad, too?

"I don't want to go back without you." I crossed my arms over my chest.

Mom sighed, a combination of sadness and regret clouding her face. "I knew this was a bad idea. I should have listened to your father . . ."

"Wait . . . what? You mean Dad knew about this?" Sure,

he knew I was a skeleton, but he never told me I could go to the Underworld and visit with my mom.

"Um-hum." Mom nodded. "He made me promise not to do it. But I didn't listen to him." She got quiet, her voice low and gloomy. "And I should have."

"Why didn't he just tell me? It would have made things so much easier. Instead, he made all these weird faces and said 'Uh, uh, uh' all the time." I paused remembering more of what Dad had said. "In fact, he told me he didn't know why you did this. He lied to me!"

"He thought it would be too hard on you. Making you say goodbye all over again."

My voice caught in my throat. "You mean I can't come back?"

"Sure you can." Mom's face brightened. "But only at night. When you're a skeleton."

"Oh," I said. "Because being a skeleton helps me blend in, right?"

"You got it."

"Well, I'm just glad Ms. Wanda helped me. Without her, I don't think I'd ever have made it to R.I.P."

"And I'm glad she followed through with her promise." Mom gazed out the window. Even though she sounded happy, her face told another story.

I slipped my hand in hers. "What's wrong?"

"You have to go now. The sun is leaving the Underworld. Soon it will rise into the Land of the Living."

"Just a few more minutes?" I wanted to whine, but I

tried to sound mature so she'd be willing to treat me like a grownup. Tantrum-throwing would definitely defeat the purpose.

"Once the sun has risen to the Land of the Living you'll be trapped here and you won't be able to get out."

"Then I'll be back first thing tomorrow."

Mom hugged me tight. "Tomorrow." She went to the shelf, scooped the cranky mouse into her palm, and placed him on my shoulder. "Time to go," she whispered to him.

"Already?" Cheddar moaned. "We just got here."

"Hurry now," she said softly. "Before it's too late."

After my mom gave me a final hug, Cheddar directed me down the cobblestone path. The sky had changed to a strange shade of gray and it made my bones ache. The neon butterflies appeared more like bats. The once beautiful pink daisies and other colorful flowers were nothing more than wilted blooms.

"Turn right," he commanded. "And make it quick, would ya? I don't want to be stuck with you in R.I.P. forever."

I patted him on the head. "Don't you worry." Even though I wanted to say something sarcastic, I stopped myself. I didn't want to be stuck with him either. That would be an eternity of awfulness. "I'll be out of here just in time."

Cheddar let out a little huff.

We turned a corner, walking around a set of tall lilac trees, their sweet fragrance tempting me to stay forever. A branch snagged on my collar bone, pulling me backward. I unhooked the limb from my bone, catching a glimpse of what appeared to be a face in the trunk. My eyes rolled around in my head—but the face disappeared when I looked again.

Ahead I saw the flashing lights of the carnival-elevator. "Hey, look." I pointed at my passage into the world of the Living. "We're here."

"Good thing," Cheddar said. "I'm getting tired of listening to your bones clatter."

I wanted to tell him that his bones weren't any quieter, but I knew it wouldn't make a difference to argue with him. "So, I'll see you tomorrow?"

The mouse scurried down my arm to my hand. "And don't be late." He curled his paw into a fist and shook it at me.

"I won't. Promise." I held my hand up in a scout's honor sign.

Cheddar scampered behind a bush and I hopped into the elevator. Ready to brace myself for a bullet-fast ride back to my world, I held on tight. But when I pressed the button for L.L. (Land of the Living) the elevator moved so slowly I almost thought it was broken. After a long time it emerged right in front of my mom's headstone.

Though the sky was still dark, I could see a hint of dawn on the horizon. It was funny how day and night were opposite each other in the real world and R.I.P. When the sun is setting in the horizon, it's really just sinking into the Underworld and lighting it up. And when it rises, it's leaving the Underworld. It was awesome for me since I'd get to experience daylight for twenty-four hours!

The sun rose faster than I thought and I ran home as fast as I could, hoping I'd make it back before my dad woke up. I didn't want to get caught—or worse, get in trouble.

No lights shone inside the house. He wasn't up. Yet. I turned the door handle, sneaking in as quietly as possible (which was hard with such noisy bones). I climbed the stairs to my room, crawled into bed, and giggled off to sleep.

A few short hours later, the smell of bacon woke me. Even though my mouth watered, my warm blankets urged me to stay in bed.

Dad walked in carrying a tray. "Morning."

For some reason his awkward smile reminded me of Mr. Peterkin. He'd had such a sheer look of terror on his face when I scared him. It was so funny, I burst out laughing.

"What is it, Lovie?"

My hands flew up to my mouth, hiding my smirk. "Nothing."

"Really?" Dad gave me a look. It was one of *those* looks. It said, *You better fess up because no one laughs like that unless they've been up to something, and when I find out what it is, you're going to be in big trouble.*

"Really." I didn't want him to know about my prank on Mr. Peterkin or my visit with Mom in R.I.P. "It's nothing." I smiled cheesily and looked at Dad wondering if he bought it.

He didn't. I knew because he still had an eyebrow lowered making his eye squint. His lips were pursed into a little bow.

With some quick thinking, I picked up a magazine and handed it to him. "Halloween. See?" I pointed to a picture of kids dressed as zombies and vampires.

"Halloween is months away." Obviously he didn't catch on at all. Dad could be so slow about things sometimes. "Is there a costume you want?"

"Da-ad. I don't need a costume." My dad's expressionless face made me burst out laughing again. "Skeleton. Remember?"

### *TIME OUT!*

*Do you have a totally clueless parent like that, too? I guess it could be a good thing—like if you ate the last piece of cake, you could deny it and they'd probably believe you. But it always seems like the times you don't want them to figure it out, they always do. Parents must have this magic thing in their brains that lets them know when their kids are up to no good. My dad says it's called experience.*

"Oh, right." He didn't laugh. Or smile for that matter. Apparently he didn't find it funny. Of course he wouldn't. He hated me as a skeleton. He was afraid and disgusted. So he probably hated thinking about Halloween and costumes and my skeleton curse. "Good point."

There was a long pause. It was uncomfortable—like that

moment when someone says something stupid and no one knows how to respond to it, so everyone gets quiet.

The silence made my heart beat out of my chest because it got me thinking. Maybe he knew about my prank on Mr. Peterkin.

Or maybe he knew that I visited Mom.

And I'm pretty sure he'd be mad about both.

"So . . . um . . . I brought you breakfast." He scratched his head, his arm, and then his face.

My stomach ached. I was sure he knew what I had been up to. "Uh, I see that, Dad."

"All right then." Dad patted my leg. He got a big crooked smile on his face. It was the kind of crooked smile that put a wrinkle in his chin. It almost looked like someone took a pencil and carved the letter *S* into his skin.

"All right, then," I echoed.

"I'm going into the office for a bit. Homework is on the counter. Call me if you need anything."

"Okay, Dad." I hugged him tightly, hoping it would remind him that I was still just his innocent, sweet little girl who could never be guilty of scaring an old man, even if he was mean and deserved it. "Have a nice day."

When Dad didn't mention anything about Mr. Peterkin or Mom, it made me think. Maybe he was acting all twitchy and crooked-smile-y because he was up to something. It made a little thing go off in my brain that said, *Dad's been acting fishy lately and we better find out what it is.*

## chapter 12

I was right.

Dad was up to something. He'd probably been up to it since the day we went shopping.

Unfortunately, I didn't have to do any snooping to find out what it was. When he came home from work he put his bag down by the door. Dad smiled so big it stretched all the way across his face, showing all of his teeth and some of his gums. He needed to floss. Badly.

"Good day?" I asked, knowing something bad was about to break loose.

Dad nodded. "I've got some great news."

Instead of answering, I just sighed. Whenever Dad had great news, it meant not such great stuff for me.

Like one time he came home with great news, and it turned out it was a half-dead goldfish he got for free. We had to flush it down the toilet later that same night when it went belly up.

Or the time he brought home a whole bag of dog food because it was free. We've never owned a dog.

Or the time he bought me a dress from a clearance rack for Aunt Sue's wedding. It was bright orange and two sizes too big. I looked like a giant pumpkin in all the photos.

Somehow Dad's great news never turned out so good for me—you can probably understand why I was a tad hesitant.

Dad sat down next to me on the couch. He held my hand and squeezed it, still smiling with this eager, cheesy grin. "I've got the answer."

"To what?"

"You've forgotten already?" Dad sighed, crossing his legs. "Your curse."

Really, I should've known. It was just a matter of time before he'd make me change. I wasn't thrilled. Being a skeleton definitely had its perks, especially since I learned I could visit my mom. There was no way I was ever, in this lifetime, going to stop visiting with her in the Underworld.

If the answer was as great as that dead goldfish, I really couldn't get super excited. "So, what's the answer?" I asked just to be nice.

Dad hesitated. He looked at me, then the floor, then back at me. He must have been pretty unsure about it for him to avoid spilling the information.

"Well, what is it?" I demanded. "A spell or something?"

Dad's caterpillar eyebrows crawled across his forehead. "Not exactly."

"Okay, not a spell." I tapped my finger to my head, thinking. "Voodoo?"

"No."

"Stop making me guess and just tell me already." Even though guessing games made me curious, they irritated me even more.

"A woman." Dad's voice cracked.

"A woman? What's so special about that?"

Dad went to the door and opened it. A woman stepped in. She wore a long skirt with big flowers on it and a turban-like twisty thing on her head.

"A fortune teller?" I slapped both my hands against my forehead and dragged them down my face. "A fortune teller is going to get rid of my curse?" My dad was so gullible.

"She swears she can help you." Dad turned to the lady. "Right, Madame Morrible?"

"Madame Morrible the horrible," I said with a giggle and an eye roll. Madame Morrible gave me a dirty look. She nodded to my dad and walked into the room, her long skirt swishing around her legs with each step. Brightly colored plastic necklaces clinked against each other. She sat on the coffee table in front of the couch, picked up my English notebook, and flipped through the pages.

After a long pause, Madame Morrible put the notebook on her lap. Her hands shot out super fast and grabbed mine, making me gasp. Her clammy hands squeezed mine and I wanted to pull away. When she resisted, my eyes focused on the ring on her index finger. The gold band had a huge orange stone in the middle of it. Her knuckles were so thick I wondered how she slipped it on.

"I see grave danger," she finally said, her voice raspy and shaky. I think she was trying to be mysterious.

Despite my best efforts, a great, big, humongous laugh burst through my nose, snot flying everywhere. I couldn't help it. I'd seen too many movies with lame fortune tellers making dumb predictions and they all had that same sound in their voices.

Without missing a beat, Madame Morrible continued. "You will meet death."

This time, I didn't try to hold in my laugh. It spilled from my mouth in a crow-like ca-caw sound.

Dad gave me a look. It said, *Cooperate with this woman or I'll see to it that her predictions come true.*

### TIME OUT!

*Am I the only one that sees the irony in that? I mean, I'm a freaking SKELETON! Well, at least at night I am. That's what's so funny about it. And everyone knows that fortune tellers just make things up. Or they ask for some personal item that would give them clues. Like a wallet or a notebook. If they could really predict the future, why don't they just use their abilities to see the next set of lottery numbers? Then they'd be millionaires and wouldn't have to go around making up stupid stuff.*

"Death and danger," Madame Morrible repeated.

All Madame Morrible had done was make stupid pre-dictions (that probably weren't even true). She hadn't done anything to change my curse. "Doesn't sound like she knows a reverse curse, Dad."

"A curse." She shot her hand into the air. "Yes, the curse! 'Tis a very bad curse."

I watched Madame Morrible's eyes scope the room. She stopped at the photo of Aunt Sue's wedding. The one with me in the orange pumpkin dress. "Yes. The curse shall turn you into a pumpkin at midnight." Madame Morrible did this thing with her voice where she tried to sound spooky, but she really just sounded like an old woman with a shaky voice.

That's when my dad started laughing, nervously. "Thank you, Madame Morrible. You've done plenty for the evening." He handed her some folded bills.

"I can reverse the pumpkin spell." She held out her hand for more money.

"Of course you can. But I think we'll live with it for a while longer." He turned and, although he winked at me, it looked more like he tried to blink away tears.

It made me realize that Dad wouldn't live with this any longer than he had to. He would definitely do everything he could to change me. Maybe he thought visiting Mom and saying goodbye every night would be too hard on me. That was nothing in comparison with how rotten he made me feel rejecting me as a skeleton. It was completely unfair that he would take it all away from me. My chest felt tight knowing he couldn't love me because I was different.

Madame Morrible handed him a business card. "Don't hesitate to call should you need anything else." She smiled and I noticed that she was missing a top tooth. "Anything," she reminded as she walked out the front door.

Once the door clicked shut, I threw a pillow at my dad. "That was great. Funny stuff." I tried to sound like I thought it was hysterical, but really I was super mad. I couldn't understand why I was hiding my real emotions from him. Was I protecting him from the same rotten feelings he gave me?

"Sorry, kiddo." He stuffed his wallet in his back pocket. "I really thought she could help."

I couldn't say anything, so I just shrugged.

Dad walked over and hugged me. I wanted to push him away, but since he thought he did something nice for me with the fortune teller thing, I gave him a wimpy kind of squeeze. "We'll find a way out of this," he said, stroking my hair. "I can't have you changing every night. It's just . . . unnatural."

"I, ah, I . . ." I wanted him to understand me for once.

"No need to thank me." Dad smiled ignorantly. "We're going to make everything normal again. I promise."

My throat squeezed tight, blocking off my air supply. I couldn't believe that my dad didn't understand how things would never be normal. Not with a daughter who was a skeleton and could visit her mom in R.I.P. I wanted to knock on his head and ask if anybody was home. Tell him that I didn't want a way out of this. Not. At. All.

## chapter 13

"Well." Dad reclined on the sofa, flipping open a newspaper. "It will be dark soon."

"And I'll be a skeleton."

Dad cringed, his shoulders pulling tight against his neck and all the muscles in his face squeezing together like he'd just sucked on a lemon. "Better get to bed."

"I know, I know," I grumbled as I started for the stairs.

"Hurry now."

Midway up the steps I stopped. "Why do I have to hurry? It's just you and me. Can't we play a game or watch a movie together?" I planted my feet and refused to take another step.

"Because it's past your bedtime." Dad let out a sigh and I could tell he really didn't want to have this conversation.

"But it's only six-thirty." I wanted to use my best whiny voice, but from the looks of it, Dad wouldn't have tolerated that very well, so I just said it nicely.

"Then don't go to sleep." Dad slapped the paper into his

lap and folded his arms abruptly. "Just go to your room." He pointed up the stairs. Dad was never stern and I could tell this was hard for him because he looked at his feet. He scratched his head. His eyebrows crawled like a caterpillar on his forehead. Then Dad did the strangest thing. He walked away. Just got up and left the room without another word.

When I heard his bedroom door click shut, I clenched my hands into tight fists. "Fine," I shouted after him, hoping if I sounded stern enough he'd know I meant business. "But we're talking about this tomorrow, mister." When Dad didn't come out of his room, not even to give me a look, I knew we wouldn't be discussing it tomorrow. Or ever, for that matter.

I moped all the way up the stairs, wishing that Dad could love me. Accept me for who I was—skeleton and all. It made my insides boil. By the time I reached my room, I was so angry I didn't care about consequences. I slammed the door and locked it. If Dad decided he wanted to talk, he'd have to knock.

Refusing to let hot tears streak down my face, I sat by my window. I watched the sky change colors as dusk settled in. I couldn't let Dad upset me so much. Mom always told me anger was a wasted emotion. Maybe she was right.

With each new color of the sunset, I felt calmer. Once the sun sank in the horizon my body transformed from Cindy to skeleton in one quick beat. It wasn't as frightening as it was before. I guess I had grown used to it. Sort of.

The phone rang and I raced to answer it.

"Hi, there," Sarah's voice greeted.

"Chicky Monkey!"

"Chickeroo," Sarah sang. "I have so much to tell you."

"I have something to tell you, too. But you go first."

I flopped back on my bed and stared at the ceiling. The crystal mobile that Mom made when I was small dangled above me, glittering against the walls. I stretched my arm out and reached for them. They seemed just out of my grasp, like everything else in my life, especially Dad's love and acceptance. A breeze stirred the mobile. It danced and lit the room with little firefly sparkles.

"Ethan asked about you."

I watched the glittering lights dance around my room, my mind wandering. "Really? That's nice." The sparkling mobile reminded me of my mom and how, before she'd tuck me in at night, we'd pretend we could fly like fairies. I was little then, but I'd never forget it. An ache in my stomach began to grow.

"Yeah. So I gave him your phone number. He's going to call you."

"Wait. What?" I shook my head, forcing myself to pay attention.

"Ethan. He's gonna call you."

"For real?"

"For real."

I jumped up and down on my bed and let out a squeal. I couldn't believe it! Ethan McCallister had my phone number and he was going to call me! "So . . . what do you think he wants?"

"I dunno. He didn't say," Sarah said. "What did you want to tell me?"

"You're never going to believe it. Not in a million years." I paused when I saw my skeleton reflection in the mirror. "Oh, um—"As much as I wanted to tell Sarah about being a skeleton and going to the Underworld, I knew I couldn't. She might be my best friend, but a skeleton curse was way too weird for anyone.

Wait . . . what was I doing talking on the phone? It was dusk and I had already transformed into a skeleton, which meant I could visit my mom! "Uh, Sarah . . . I have to go. I'll tell you all about it tomorrow. 'Kay?" But it was a lie. I'd never be able to tell her.

"Uh . . . okay. Tomorrow, Chickeroo."

"Tomorrow. I promise." Before she hung up, I quickly said, "And thanks for . . . the Ethan thing. You're the best." Then I clicked the phone off and raced out the front door. Thankfully, since Dad had sulked off to his bedroom earlier, he wasn't there to stop me. He was so disgusted by me as a skeleton he probably didn't care what I did anyway.

I ran to the cemetery without stopping.

Cheddar tapped his foot and pointed to the moon. "You're late."

"I'm sorry. I got here as fast as I could."

"Well, let's not drag this out any longer than we have to." He motioned for me to pick him up. I bent down and he jumped on my hand, scurrying up my arm. He settled on my shoulder with a *humpf*. "Now let's go."

With Cheddar huffing so loud it echoed in my skull, I stepped inside the hot pink elevator. The magical transport shot into the ground like a bullet.

When we stepped out of the elevator and into R.I.P., my body tingled; I was so excited to see my mom. Without thinking I raced ahead, not paying any attention to the path. I ran so fast, I missed the ticket booth. Even though I should have been worried about getting caught, I was just too eager to spend time with my mom.

"Hey! You! R.D.—you need a ticket!"

I stopped, turning to see who shouted. It was Bert. I recognized his Yankee baseball cap and his shirt with the name badge on the pocket.

"Oh, sorry. I forgot," I said, backing up. But my burst of excitement was replaced with fear as soon as I saw Bert's face. Pieces of his skin were flaking off along his jaw. Bruises around his dark eyes made him look tired. And dead. I shivered, my bones making a strange rattling noise.

Cheddar passed Bert two gold coins, just like he had before, and in exchange Bert gave him two tickets.

The tension floated thick in the air. Did Bert know I wasn't an R.D.? And why was his face decaying?

Bert shoved a cigar into his mouth. "Hv-A-Nc-Dy." He gave me a look when he said it. The look said, *I know something is going on here and I don't like it.*

When we were far enough away Cheddar tapped my shoulder. "You have to be careful."

"Yep. I know." I felt like dark clouds were descending on

us. The bright purple sky didn't look as beautiful as it did before. And the turquoise astro turf looked more like half-dead weeds.

"Are things . . . different? The Underworld seems—"

"Nope. Just move along. Everything's fine. And remember the rules!"

I nodded then skipped ahead. But I stayed more aware of my surroundings than ever. In fact, I swore I saw hundreds of eyes on the edge of the grass. They blinked and winked at me. They followed each step I took. My bones rattled with nervousness. If I had skin, it would have been covered in goose bumps instead. I rubbed my boney skeleton hands against my eyes. When I looked again, there were just fireflies skittering around.

"We're almost there," Cheddar said. I know he was trying to reassure me, but it almost sounded like he said it for himself.

As soon as we arrived at the gate, I felt better. "Cinderella," Mom sang, rushing out to greet me.

We hugged tight. When she pulled away she looked into my eyes, sensing with her mom-powers that something was wrong. "You okay? Seems like something's gotten to you."

At first I shook my head, but as we headed into the house and I stood there in the warm, familiar surroundings, I felt safe confiding in her. "Things seem different in R.I.P."

"Well, of course they are. It's not the Land of the Living." She took Cheddar off my shoulder and placed him in a basket on the kitchen counter. For once, he snuggled in and went to sleep.

"No, that's not it. I mean it seems different than yesterday. When I went through the ticket booth, I noticed that parts of Bert's face were decaying and . . . ." I paused, thinking back to my journey along the path. "There were eyes . . . I swear something was watching me."

"Hmmmm . . ." Mom tapped her finger on her chin. "We'll have to be more careful. The Underkeeper has rules. And they must not be broken."

"About the Living in R.I.P.?" My bones trembled. I wanted this to be a fun visit, but I felt scared.

"Yes, that's one of them." Mom brushed a strand of hair off her face. "We don't need to worry about any of that right now. I have a movie planned." She reached toward the table then held up the latest scary movie. "Thought you'd like to see this one."

"How'd you get that?" I couldn't believe she had it already. The movie wasn't even in theaters yet.

"Those of us in the Underworld . . . we have ways." Mom winked at me.

"Sa-weet." I plopped on the sofa and Mom put on the movie.

Mom sat next to me, placing a fuzzy blanket on my lap. Scruffy leapt onto the back of the couch purring. He rubbed his skull on my shoulder. I patted him until he decided to curl up on the sofa next to me. "Did you have any problems getting here?"

Other than nearly skipping the ticket booth and Bert's decaying skin? Creepy eyes and half-dead grass? "Not at all," I said.

"So Dad didn't give you a hard time?"

My mouth fell open wide and I gave her the best skeleton look I could. It said, *Oh, shoot! I'm in trouble. I was supposed to tell Dad?*

"You didn't tell him, did you?"

I shook my head. "Un-uh."

"Cin-dy," she said in that scolding mom-voice.

"We had a fight, so it's not like he'd listen to me or anything. All he wants to do is change me. He hates that I'm a skeleton. He doesn't even love me anymore."

"I had no idea." Mom's eyes glazed over. "Give him some time—he'll adjust."

"It's fine." I shrugged. The last thing I wanted was for my mom to feel guilty. I'd deal with Dad on my own.

We settled in on the couch, ready for a fun night of movie viewing. When the creepy music started, I inched closer. At the first sign of a scary part, Mom pulled the blanket up over her eyes. I ducked underneath and put my hands where my ears would have been. Then we giggled about how silly we were.

As soon as the movie ended, Mom bolted into the kitchen. "How about some dinner? You've got to be starving. I know I am."

"You don't have to—"

"Nonsense. I want to." Mom got busy pulling out pots and

pans, herbs, and spices. She cooked a gourmet meal with all my favorite foods: peas, mashed potatoes with gravy, and pot roast. It filled the house with a warm, inviting aroma. Just like when she was alive.

We sat down to eat but when I swallowed a bite, it fell into my lap. Mom saw all the chewed-up food piled there and laughed. "Guess I didn't think that through very well."

"It's okay. I don't mind. Not really." I smiled for her.

Mom smiled back but the sparkle in her eyes was gone.

After we cleaned up the dinner dishes, Mom served chocolate cake with ice cream for dessert. It was a good thing I couldn't feel hot or cold because I had a feeling that if I could, the ice cream would have made me prance around the room once it hit my bones.

Mom gave me a towel to clean up and I scuttled off to the bathroom. When I returned she pointed outside. "It's getting late." She took my hands in hers and knelt in front of me. "You know I'll always be here, right?" Her voice sounded higher than usual and I couldn't understand why she might be feeling sad.

"Yup, I know that. That's why you can bet I'll be back. I wouldn't miss seeing you again for the world." We hugged and then, with Cheddar on my shoulder, I raced to the elevator.

I didn't see any pairs of eyes on the side of the path. Still, I had an uncanny feeling that someone—or something—was watching me.

## chapter 14

Afer another slow ride up to the cemetery, I said goodbye to Cheddar and went home as fast as I could.

I made it back to my room just as the sun began to rise. My body transformed from the skeleton into me, Cindy-skeleton. Because I was part Cindy, part skeleton. But then I thought about my mom, our fun visit, and how she always calls me Cinderella. I decided the best name would be Cinderskella. I couldn't wait to share my new name with my mom. I bet she'd love it.

I fell asleep for a few hours and, when I woke up, I suddenly remembered my conversation with Sarah. Maybe Ethan really would call me!

When I went downstairs for breakfast, Dad had already gone to work. There was a note on the counter. It said,

*If you're up to it, you should try going to school today. And*

*some boy named Ethan called this morning. He has your math notebook.*

My stomach sank. That was it? This big exciting message from Ethan was about a math notebook?

As disappointed as I was with the lame message, seeing Dad's note made me think about our fight. I crumpled up the paper and tossed it, aiming for the garbage, but missed.

Even if Dad was right, and I should return to school, I didn't feel ready. There would be too many questions from my friends and their friends. And there would definitely be too many sad looks from the teachers.

Plus, if the teachers ever found out about my visits to R.I.P. they probably wouldn't believe me and they'd send me to talk to the guidance counselor. Then they'd tell my dad which would cause BIG problems. So, I'd have to fake being sad and I was pretty sure I wasn't a good faker.

I went to the front door and rifled through my backpack. When I found my science book, I scanned the next chapter. It was all about the life cycle of the butterfly. That seemed so first grade to me. But then I thought about how much my curse reminded me of butterflies. You see, they change too. They start off as ugly wormy caterpillar things, and after being wrapped up for a while, they turn into something beautiful. And that's what I did every day. The beautiful part being that I could visit my mom, of course.

My stomach growled. Being a skeleton definitely made me hungry. All that food in the Underworld didn't stay with me very well since it just fell out below my ribs. I went to the kitchen and opened the fridge. Nothing. Even the pantry was empty. I had no choice. I dug around in the kitchen drawer for the emergency fund envelope. I was hungry. There were no groceries. That definitely constituted an emergency.

Money in hand, I walked to the corner market—Imma's Real Boy. I knew exactly what I wanted. A bag of sour cream and onion potato chips and a roast beef sub. But when I went to the chip aisle, all they had were dill pickle flavored potato chips and a few bags of plain ones. If you ask me, anything pickled is worse than gross—it's disgusting! Once, I saw a jar of pickled eggs and almost barfed. Who would come up with something so unnatural anyway?

I settled for a bag of plain chips, found a pre-made sub, and went to the counter and paid for it. The man who ran the store was named Pin, though mom said I had to call him Mr. Occhio out of respect. He had balding hair and stood slightly taller than me. Whenever he smiled, his eyes did too. He spoke in broken English most of the time.

"Ah, Cindy. Nice to see you. Every-sing going well, yes?" He smiled widely. Mr. Occhio was always smiling. I swore he had never been sad as long as I'd known him.

"It's fine," I said. "It'd be better if you had sour cream and onion." I held up the bag of potato chips.

"Sorry. All out." He shrugged. When I paid him, he handed me a lollipop. "Want candy? Sorry 'bout no sour cream chips for you."

I took the pop and stuck it in my pocket. "That's okay. Thanks, Mr. Occhio!" The door chimed behind me as I left.

When I got home, I sat on the couch with my lunch, not caring about getting the crumbs on the sofa cushions. I had only taken a couple bites of my deli sub when Dad carried in two large bags of groceries, placing them on the kitchen counter. Good thing, too, because my sandwich was soggy, like the bread had been sitting in water instead of the refrigerator at the deli.

Maybe Dad had something better. I stuck my arm in one of the grocery sacks and dug around. He tapped my shoulder but I ignored him and kept digging for a snack. Dad huffed and, when I finally looked at him, I noticed something different. An expression I hadn't seen before.

"Cindy." His face was pale and I thought he would vomit. Maybe that's what the look was. He was sick.

"Yeah, Dad?" There was a box of granola bars at the bottom of the bag. Chocolate chip. I pulled it out, tore open the box, and started eating one.

"I want you to meet someone."

"Oh," I said, with a full mouth of yumminess. But I really thought, *This ought to be good.* The last someone was a fortune teller. Maybe this time it was a tarot card reader, or a palm reader. Better yet, maybe it was a ghost whisperer. Now that would be super cool.

I stuffed the rest of the bar in my mouth. "So, who do you want me to meet?" I asked while I chewed and chomped.

Dad swallowed hard.

Something about his hesitation caught my attention. I stopped chewing and chomping and stared at him. "Well?"

Dad looked like he'd seen a ghost.

"Seriously." The anticipation built in my gut like a volcano ready to explode. "Who is it?"

I watched as he gathered his strength, straightening his tie and clearing his throat. "Your new mother," he blurted out.

You know that moment when you swear your heart stops beating? And your breath comes in these shallow little waves? Well, that's exactly what I felt like, except like a gazillion times worse. "I'm sorry. What did you say?" I was sure I hadn't heard him correctly.

"Your new mother," Dad said with a nervous laugh.

A wave of heat flooded my body and it went from my head to my toes and back up again, stopping at my face and burning like a furnace. Instead of listening to anything else my dad might have to say, I marched out of the kitchen, straight upstairs to my room.

What was wrong with him? First he kept secrets, then he was disgusted by me, now he was marrying another woman?

Dad knocked on my door. "You need to come out." He stepped inside my room, even though it should have been obvious by the barricade of pillows and chairs that I didn't want visitors.

"I don't want to." I buried my face in a pillow. If I had to look at him I might have screamed. Or thrown something.

He put his hand on my shoulder. "But you need to meet her." My dad sounded like a robot, like he couldn't even think for himself.

I didn't want to meet her. Why did I need a new mother? Why couldn't I just have my own mom? I moved the pillow, staring Dad down. "You mean this isn't a horrible, terrible nightmare and I'm not going to wake up screaming any minute?"

Dad shook his head.

"So, this is real? She's here?"

The doorbell rang and I sat up in a start, my face crinkled with anger.

"That would be her now." Dad smoothed my hair. "She'll be a great mother. I promise."

I shot him a look, my eyes like lasers. Although the look should have been enough, I actually said it aloud. "I don't care how great you think she is. She'll *never* be my mother. No one will ever be my mother except Mom."

"She'll be good to you, Cindy."

My body shook with anger. I couldn't understand why my dad would have replaced my mom so fast. "Why would you do this?"

Dad shot me a look. I can't tell you how bad the look was. Let's just say, if his eyes could spit fire, the room would be an inferno.

I shrank a little. "What's the hurry?"

Dad had a faraway gaze in his eyes. "She has daughters your age. You'll go to school together. Maybe you'll even

be in some of the same classes." Instead of sounding like a robot now, he sounded hopeful. "I think you'll be good friends," he said matter-of-factly.

Yeah, right. Like those girls would ever be my friends. "You read my mind," I said with my best sa-ttitude voice (that's sarcasm and attitude smooshed together).

Dad went downstairs. I heard the door open and voices floated into my room. A few minutes later, Dad was back. "Let's go." He gestured with a tip of his head. Begrudgingly I agreed and he gently led me out of my room, down the stairs to the living room. Although I really wanted to kick and scream, I didn't. Instead, I calmly made my way downstairs with my arms crossed. Maybe because I was in shock. Maybe because I was in denial. Or maybe it was just because I felt so numb. I barely had time to adjust to the whole skeleton thing, and now this?

When we reached the living room there were suitcases strewn on the floor.

"Hagatha," Dad said trying to bridge the awkward gap between us. "This is my daughter, Cindy."

Hagatha snaked forward until her face invaded my bubble of personal space.

I clenched my teeth so hard my jaw ached. And my mouth clamped so tight that my lips were drawn into a thin line with the corners pointed down.

"Well, haven't we a long face," my new mother said. Strands of her mousy brown hair swayed in place as she crossed her arms.

Her daughters laughed. Both of the girls had the same straight brown hair as their mother.

I gave Hagatha a look, uncrossing my arms and clenching fists at my side. It said, *Don't mess with me 'cause I'm not in the mood for it.*

My new mother glared at me. Obviously she didn't like my "look."

"Not quite as long as yours," I said, eyeing her hideously oblong face, her chin protruding like a lemon.

My new mother narrowed her green eyes, disapproving. "I see I've got my work cut out for me." She held her hands out to her daughters like she was the lead on a leash. "Come, girls. Let's find our rooms." She snaked up the stairs, her daughters trailing behind. The girls' footsteps creaked on the wood floors overhead. But I heard Hagatha's feet slithering.

Turning to Dad, I rolled my eyes. "I thought they were girls, not dogs."

"Cindy," Dad said. "Be nice."

"Fine." I crossed my arms again. "I just don't understand why I have to have a new mother already."

"You'll understand in time." Dad turned away, and all of a sudden I knew there was something much more to all of this. Something that he wasn't telling me.

## chapter 15

"Mom wouldn't approve," I mumbled under my breath.

"What was that?"

"Nothing."

Dad grabbed my hand. "What did you say about Mom?"

"Nothing, all right?" I pulled away, but Dad's gaze broke me down into a blob of confessing Jell-o. "Fine. I just said that Mom's not going to like this."

Dad's eyes grew huge. "You've been sneaking out and visiting her, haven't you?"

I gulped. Parents. Always. Know.

"I told her not to do . . . I can't believe . . ." Dad paced around the living room, sweat beading on his upper lip. "How could she . . . When . . . What was she thinking?" He ran his fingers through his hair, pulling out a few strands on the way. "It's dangerous, Cindy!"

"Don't worry, Dad." I tried to be calm for his sake. But it

didn't help. "I've been careful. Besides, there isn't anything dangerous about R.I.P."

Dad suddenly stopped pacing. He clenched his teeth together and folded his arms across his chest. "Seems I brought Hagatha here just in time."

Huh? Did he bring her here to stop me from seeing my mom? This new mother would ruin my life. I knew it.

At dinner I was forced to sit between my stepsisters. I felt like I couldn't breathe. Had it not been for the roast chicken and pasta, I would have gone to my room and stayed there permanently.

I figured if my new mother was like the fairy tale Cinderella's stepmother, I would be forced into a life of servitude and I'd get stuck washing dishes.

But she didn't make me wash a single one.

### TIME OUT!

*I know what you're thinking. You thought she was going to be a mean stepmother and that getting out of washing dishes doesn't sound mean to you. But just you wait, you'll see. She gets really mean.*

While I had the chance, I snuck out of the kitchen, went to my room, and locked myself inside, ready to stay there forever and never be bothered by my new mother or her daughters again. I wasn't going to be nice. Even if she did let me off the hook with dishwashing duty.

I knew Dad wouldn't make me come out of my room since he was embarrassed about my skeleton curse. So, I was safe. At least until morning.

As soon as everyone was asleep, I snuck downstairs, avoiding suitcases and all the junk Hagatha, my so-called new-mother, and her daughters had brought with them. Once I navigated the maze, I dashed through the front door. I couldn't believe my good luck! New-mother didn't wake up. And since my dad wasn't anywhere to be seen, he didn't try to stop me either.

I knew it was cold out by the way the trees shivered in the breeze. It was another time I was glad to be a skeleton. Plus, I didn't have any hair, so it wasn't blowing in my face and getting tangled. Talk about a major mess to comb out later.

At the cemetery I waited near my mom's headstone, but there was no sign of Cheddar. I traced my hand over the slab searching for a button. Nothing. I stomped around the grave. No elevator. Maybe no one would come for me tonight. The thought made me feel sad and scared. I trembled so hard my bones sounded like dried beans in a glass dish.

"CHED-DAR!" My bones rattled in the wind, drowning out my voice. "CHEEEED-DAAAR!" I paced, my skeleton feet slapping against the ground with each step. What if my mom didn't want to see me anymore? What if something happened and I couldn't go back to see her ever again? I don't think I could live with that.

All hope lost, I slumped on the ground next to my mom's

grave. I put my hands to my face, letting the waterworks flow. My sobs echoed so loud they whipped around the headstone right back to my skull.

Cheddar sluggishly crawled out of a small hole behind my mom's headstone. "All right," he said. "What seems to be the problem?"

I scooped the mouse up and leapt to my feet. "You're here!"

"Yeah, yeah. And you're late. Again. You're lucky I came back."

"I know." I hung my head. "It's not really my fault . . . I have a stepmother."

"Sorry to hear that," Cheddar said in his most sympathetic voice, which wasn't really sympathetic at all. "Now let's get going before our time is up. Nothing worse than a wasted trip to R.I.P." He jumped from my hand and landed on my mom's grave. The elevator shot out of the ground.

"How do you do that?"

"Magic," he said, clinking his giant front teeth together. "Your mother is one smart witch."

Of course. How could I be so silly?

After another gravity-defying trip in the elevator, we stopped at the ticket booth. Bert was there, again. At least I thought it was Bert because he wore the same Yankees cap and had the same dark eyes. But there was no more skin on his face and one eye dangled out of its socket. Bert was a skeleton!

"Two tickets," Cheddar said in a huff.

Bert slid the tickets across the counter. "Wait a minute." He jerked the tickets back, his eyeball jostling. "Haven't you been here before?" he asked, eyeing me suspiciously, the one hanging from the socket, swaying back and forth. Actually I don't know if it was suspicious—without skin, his other eye just rolled around in his head. Kind of like mine.

I started to nod, but Cheddar flicked the side of my skull with his paw. "Uh, nope," he said. "She's an R.D."

Bert tapped his finger to his head. "Hmmm . . . something's fishy here. R.D.s aren't skeletons. They can't be. It takes a while to decompose. I mean, look at me."

"Well, this one got lost along the way." Cheddar said it so surely I almost believed him.

"Fine." Bert pushed the tickets toward Cheddar. "But if I see you bring another skeleton through here I'm contacting the Undertaker."

"Whatever you say." Cheddar grabbed the tickets.

Bert lit a cigar and placed it in his mouth. "Hv-a-nc-dy."

"Hurry," Cheddar whispered. The way he said it—all breathy and nervous—scared me.

I ran at full-speed all the way down the cobblestone path, until we arrived at my mom's little cottage.

"Cinderella," Mom called as she saw me. "How'd it go today?"

I didn't want to tell her about my run-in with Bert. Or that I'd almost been caught, so I changed the subject. "Great. What you got planned tonight?" Mom scanned the yard then took my hand and quickly led me inside. There was no joyous reunion with hugs and stuff, just a rushed effort to bring me indoors. Which was okay with me.

"Everything all right?" I asked.

"Absolutely," Mom said.

"No, it's not," Cheddar chimed in.

Mom scooped Cheddar off my shoulder, placing him in a basket on the kitchen counter. "Just, uh, happy to see you, is all. Why don't you have a seat?"

Before I could sit down Mom raced around the house closing all the shutters and locking the doors. She was obviously nervous. But I wasn't about to let her know I felt nervous about her being nervous, which was possibly due to me being nervous about her being nervous.

My favorite game sat on the coffee table, set up and ready to go. There were mugs of hot cocoa and a plate of chocolate chip cookies.

My eyes grew wide and I nearly forgot about all my troubles. "This is going to be great."

"I thought you'd like it." She smiled warmly, with a slight nervous twitch. "Be careful with the cocoa though. It's pretty hot."

"That's not a problem, remember?" I pointed to my skeleton self.

Mom giggled. "Right. Sorry about that."

I chomped into a cookie. Crumbs fell from my mouth ... and my ribcage. "Happens all the time." I tried to wink but instead my eyeball just twitched.

Mom started the game by rolling the dice. She drew a

card, read it aloud, then moved her token. We took turns like this for a while. But I started thinking about how much I didn't want to go back home and it spoiled my mood. This was my real home. Plus I had that stepmother and her daughters to deal with at my dad's house. I slumped back against the sofa, the weight of the Underworld weighing on my shoulders.

Mom noticed the change in my mood. "Are you okay?"

"Just . . . thinking about my next move . . . in the game." I didn't want to upset her.

Mom wasn't going for it. "You can tell me." She inched closer, putting her arm around my boney shoulder. "Nothing is so bad that you can't tell me."

She was right. I had to get this off my chest. "I have a stepmother," I blurted out. As soon I said it, I felt bad. Mom didn't need to be bothered with my problems and she most definitely didn't need to be hurt, knowing that Dad had betrayed her. Still, I couldn't keep it bottled up anymore.

"You do?"

"I'm sorry . . . I shouldn't have told you." I turned to see if she was hurt by the news.

A relieved smile grew on her face and her eyes lit. She looked like she would burst with joy. "That's wonderful!"

"What?" I sat up, breaking her hug. "How is that good? She's awful and horrible!"

Mom let out a chuckle. I don't know what she found so funny about it. "I bet she's not that bad."

I tried to give my mom a look, but instead my eyeballs just rolled around. "So, you're not angry about this?"

"No, Cindy. Why should I be?"

"He replaced you." I wanted to growl in outrage. How could she not see how horrible this was? Why wasn't she upset?

She shook her head. "No, not replaced . . ."

"Then what is it?"

Mom reached across the table and smoothed my boney hand. "Your dad's a smart man. A good, smart man."

"So?" I shrugged.

"I think you should just try to cooperate." Mom turned away and walked to the fireplace. She kept her back to me, so I couldn't see her face. But I swore her voice got all shaky. Kind of like that sound when someone cries about something that makes them happy but sort of sad at the same time. I think my mom once called it bittersweet. "Dad knows what he's doing. I promise."

"Fine. But I won't be nice about it."

She went to the kitchen and poured me another cup of cocoa. She placed it on the table and sat back down on the sofa. We polished off the rest of the cookies and drank our cocoa in silence. When I had quite the puddle gathered, Mom sopped it up with a towel.

"Sorry about the mess." I tried to smile sheepishly, but my teeth just clinked together.

"Don't you worry about it. It's no problem at all." She looked alarmed, eyes growing wide, her breath catching in her throat. "It's time. You have to go." She gazed at the changing sky.

"I know." I didn't want to say goodbye. For some reason I felt like if I did, it would be my last one. "See you tomorrow."

Mom gave me this small smile where she drew her lips tight, almost like she was trying to hold back tears. She gathered up Cheddar, placing him on my shoulder.

"You disturbed my nap," he whined.

"Time for another trip," I said, patting his head.

He yawned. "Already?" But then his eyes bulged when he saw the color of the sky—a dull gray. "Let's go."

Cheddar and I hurried back to the elevator, the color of the sky making me feel uneasy. What was happening in R.I.P?

"Get in. Quickly!" Cheddar demanded.

I hopped into the elevator, pressed a button, and made the slow ascent into the cemetery. When I looked through the glass I saw Cheddar scurry away, faster then I'd ever seen him move.

When I reached the cemetery, I let out a breath. I guess I didn't know I'd been holding it. I raced home—the sound of my boney feet clunking against the pavement—feeling like I was being watched.

Thankfully, I made it home—safe and sound—before anyone woke up. Or before whatever watched me from the graveyard had a chance to do anything about it.

I forced myself to go to sleep even though I wasn't tired. I didn't want to think about all the stuff I'd seen in the Underworld. And I didn't want to face the changes in my family. My dad. New-mother. My stepsisters.

# Cindershella

When I got up the next morning I decided to go to school. Anything would be better than staying home and enduring my new so-called family. So I got dressed then went to the kitchen for breakfast. My stepsisters were sitting at the table, scarfing cereal like they hadn't eaten in days, milk splattering as they slurped away.

"Could you make a bigger mess?" I handed them a roll of paper towels.

One sister—the taller of the two—smiled, her teeth in desperate need of braces. She nudged her sister, who stopped slurping long enough to peek at me over the rim of her bowl.

"Morning, Cindy," the taller sister said. "Winnie," she said, pointing to herself. "And this is Bertha." Winnie pointed at her sister—a short, dumpy girl.

Bertha didn't smile, so I couldn't tell if she needed braces too, but she definitely could have used some zit cream.

Winnie furrowed her brow, her eyes crossing and her face looking like she was in a great deal of pain. "So, you going to school today?" Her voice sounded like a cat whose tail had been stepped on.

I poured myself some cereal. I refused to answer stupid questions.

"Want to walk together?" she asked. Winnie didn't seem to get the fact that I was ignoring them.

Nearly choking on my cereal, I looked at her, rolling my eyes. "I think I can handle it."

"Suit yourself." At that, Bertha took Winnie by the arm, they grabbed their books, and left.

When I finished eating I carried my dishes to the sink and started washing them. Then I realized that I had a step-mother to wash dishes, so I turned the water off and walked away from the sink.

I didn't need to wash dishes. What I really needed was to go to school. Ready to leave, I picked up my backpack by the front door—exactly where I had dropped it the afternoon Mom died.

The only thing different about my school since the last time I saw it was the big sign over the front door that said,

*Join us for the Spring Fling, Friday, 7 o'clock. A dance to remember!*

At the same time that I noticed the sign, my BFF Sarah came racing to me. "Chickeroo." She tackled me with a hug.

"Chicky Monkey. I missed you."

"I missed you, too." She studied my face a minute, before adding, "Are you okay?"

Which meant she knew about my mom's funeral. "I'm fine." I smiled, hoping she'd understand that I didn't want to talk about it.

She pointed to the sign. "So, want to go?" That was the best thing about her. Even though she was willing to listen, she could always take the hint and just move on like nothing ever happened.

"Might be fun." Secretly I didn't want to tell her that I was super excited because maybe Ethan would finally notice me. And maybe he'd even call me and ask me to go. Instead of leaving a lame message about my notebook. And maybe I wouldn't have to come up with another failed Operation Something-another.

"Maybe you can go with Ethan McCallister."

I gave her a look. It said, *Is there a microphone in my head?*

When I got home from school, I knew I would need to beg with every ounce of my average middle-school (translation: BORING) life for permission to go to the dance. Dad's rule stated that I had to be twelve, and at eleven and three-quarters it probably wouldn't matter much to my dad that I already *felt* twelve. Fat chance he'd break the rules and let me go. But, maybe he'd change his mind just this once if I coaxed him. Or if I looked really pathetic, puppy dog eyes and all.

Dad sat at the table, his arms crossed. It seemed he crossed his arms a lot lately. "A dance?"

"Yeah, Friday. Can I go?"

Winnie laughed and it sounded like a horse. Her crooked teeth stuck out in a bad overbite. Her mouth opened wide with each bray. I wondered if that's how she got her name. Dad turned toward my new mother, Hagatha. My fate rested in her hands. How was that even fair? Why did she get to make decisions about my life? She wasn't my real mother. I couldn't bring myself to look at her, forcing my eyes to stay focused on my plate of food.

"She can go," I heard Hagatha say. My heart skipped a beat. Maybe she wasn't so horrible after all! I snapped my eyes up just in time to see Hagatha looking at her daughters. An evil grin spread across her face. "But she has some chores to do first."

Winnie and Bertha laughed like they knew what my new mother was thinking.

"Chores?" I asked, trying not to let my voice choke. Okay, I wasn't entirely opposed to work. I did my fair share of chores when my mom was alive, but I wasn't about to become the housemaid or something.

"Yes, dear child." New-mother's voice sang the words in a high pitch sound that grated on my nerves. "Chores." She paced behind me. Hagatha seemed like a vulture circling, and I was the prey. A rabbit maybe, running as fast as its little legs could go. "They're good for you."

Yes, I was definitely the prey because I was already a goner. I gulped. Hard.

She stared me down, her eyes blazing. "Maybe you'll learn a thing or two."

Learn a thing or two? What did she mean by that? I figured it was stepmom talk for, *You'll be a better person for helping out, and if you don't change, I'll eat you for supper.*

## chapter 16

I couldn't wait to visit my mom. Once she heard about how my stepmother was making me do chores in order to go to the dance, she'd have something to say about it. For sure.

Cheddar sat atop my mom's headstone. "What do you want?"

"Uh—"

"That's what I thought." Cheddar humpfed and, with a giant leap, landed on my shoulder. "Get going already, would you? I haven't got all day."

As quick as a wink the elevator spat us out into the Underworld. We approached the ticket booth and, lucky for me, Bert had the day off.

When we came to the fork in the road, I noticed the dark, creepy path again. I hadn't paid much attention to it since my first trip to R.I.P. Usually I was just so excited to see my mom. But today I stopped and stared down that path. In a strange way, it called to me.

I turned and took one step in the direction of the darkness. Trees stretched out, their branches like claws. Strange birds with feathers as heavy as stone cawed in the tree tops. Voices whispered, their sounds haunting me. There were more piles of—*gulp*—bones scattered along the path.

"Turn around," Cheddar grunted. "Then keep moving. In the *right* direction. You know the way."

I might not have had skin, but I swore goose bumps spread across my bones. "Fine with me," I lied. One of these times I was going to see what was down there.

"The Living. Gotta tell them every single thing. Nothing but a nuisance, if you ask me."

We reached my mom's cottage and I flung open the gate on her fence and raced straight inside. I told her all about Hagatha and her horrid plans to make me do chores.

"Can you believe it?" I said to my mom as I placed Cheddar in his basket. He humpfed his usual irritated noise before curling into a ball. I held my breath waiting for Mom's shocked response.

Scruffy weaved between Mom's legs, meowing loudly. "All right. Dinner's coming." She bent down and scratched the top of his skull between where his ears would have been. Mom then shoved a casserole in the oven. After that she turned to me, brushing a strand of hair from her face. "Now, what was it you were saying?"

"Hagatha . . . chores . . ."

"Oh, right. Of course. Well, Cindy, I think you should listen to her." She went back to working in the kitchen, not looking at me.

"Mothers always know best."

"But she's not my mom." I crossed my arms, frustrated.

"You are."

"I know. And I always will be. But—"

"But what?" Why wasn't she being reasonable? This definitely wasn't the response I expected. "But you think I should just do everything I'm supposed to and not even question it?"

"Some things are better left unquestioned."

If I hadn't been a skeleton, my blood would have been boiling. "Why won't you take my side? I mean, it's like you'd rather agree with a complete horrible stranger!" I wanted to throw a massive, elephant-sized tantrum, but I clenched my hands into fists so I'd stay calm. For her.

Mom sighed a big, long, deep breath. She took my hand in hers. "We all love you, Cindy. We just want what's best for you."

Why did she always have to be so positive? I ducked my head, fiddling with a bone in my thumb. "I know."

Mom placed a hand on my shoulder, giving it a squeeze. She walked around to my side, knelt down, cradling my jaw in her hands. "Why don't you go back home and get some sleep? Do your chores and I bet things will be better than you thought."

A sob built in my chest, but it just seeped out between my ribs. "If you say so." It wasn't what I wanted to hear—or what I wanted to admit—but if it would make my mom happy, I would do it. But only for her.

Mom kissed my skull. "Let's wake Cheddar so he can guide you back."

"We don't need to do that. I know my way. Besides, he was really cranky today. I think all this traveling is making him tired or something."

"All right then. But take this." She handed me a black iron key with a long shank and a swirly curlicue loop on the end.

"What's this?"

"A skeleton key. It will unlock the elevator."

"Oh," I said, sucking in air on the "oh" because I'd just been presented with a magnificent token. Maybe I wouldn't have to deal with Cheddar anymore. Though, I think I'd miss the little rat.

I started down the cobblestone path, watching as Mom stood on the front step and waved. "See you soon," she called. "Be safe." She rubbed her hands against her arms like she was cold.

I waved goodbye and kept walking.

The sky hadn't started changing yet, so the Underworld was still in full daylight. Without Cheddar to annoy me, I had as much time as I wanted to get back to the elevator.

The air smelled delicious, like buttery popcorn and sweet candied apples. I didn't want to leave the Underworld just yet.

Without much thought, I strayed from the main path, wandering into the meadow. I skipped and pranced through the grass. The flowers were so beautiful and I'd always wanted to keep some, so I reached down to break the stem of a flower and thought I saw an eye blink in the grass. Startled, I jumped back, stepping on something mushy. Stumbling onto the cobblestones, I lifted my foot and saw an eyeball stuck between my toes. "Ugh!" I flicked it away and it rolled into the meadow. "Gross."

Not wanting to step on any more eyes, I stayed on the path. Before long, I reached the fork in the road. I pondered my choices: the carnival, home, or darkness. For the first time, I felt like I had control. No stepmother making me do chores, no dad forcing me to be nice, and no mom instructing me to cooperate. There was no one telling me what I should do. Not even Cheddar.

The dark trees called to me. What if I just took a tiny peek?

*No way.* I shook my head. I couldn't do that. What if something horrible and terrible happened? I should just go the way I was supposed to—home. I shouldn't stray. It was one of the rules.

But I'd gone into the meadow and nothing bad happened. Well, I stepped on an eyeball, but that wasn't a big deal, was it?

My fingers gripped the key tighter. I just had to have an itty-bitty peek down that creepy path. The rest of R.I.P. seemed so happy. My super-sleuthing detective impulses just had to know why it was different. Cheddar had only told me to stay on the path. Technically, I was still on a path. He just didn't have to know which one.

I would just go for a short while, until I saw whatever it was I wanted to see, then I'd go right home. My mom would never know.

I clutched the key tight in my hand. If I'd been normal-Cindy, it would have slid out because I'm sure my skin would have been sweating like mad. Good thing I was a skeleton. Turning, I started down the dark, strangled-tree path.

I took a step. Then one more. The beautiful lavender sky of R.I.P. disappeared and dark clouds hovered above me like a heavy blanket. A few more steps in and darkness surrounded me. Strange noises echoed through the forest. Whispers floated around me, their sounds slinking between my bones.

A few more steps. I wasn't a chicken, even if people did tell me I had chicken legs. A crow flew overhead and perched on a tree limb. It flapped its wings, a couple of feathers falling to the ground heavy like rocks. The bird watched me, its beady red eyes reminding me that I wasn't supposed to be here. He cawed loudly, alerting a flock of fellow crows. They swooped in, flapping their wings, a shower of rocks raining down on me.

"Stupid birds. Go away!" My bones rattled even though I told myself I wasn't scared. "This isn't worth it," I whispered. Even if there was something interesting down that path, those pesky birds would pummel me to death with their stupid stony feathers.

"What's not?" a voice called from behind.

I spun around. Unfortunately, I was so far down the dark path that all I could see was a shadowy figure, backlit by the beautiful sky of the Underworld. And blinking eyes in the grass.

The figure stepped closer until we were nearly face to face. A clownish-looking old man stood before me.

Did I ever tell you that clowns totally freak me out? Well, they do. My feet leapt so high in the air, the rest of me couldn't keep up and I clattered to the ground in a heap of bones.

Gulping, I gathered myself together.

The clown-man was dressed entirely in shades of gray, his shirt like a patchwork quilt. His face was painted white but I could see his skin was wrinkled with age. No big nose though and no big red smile or stars around his eyes. Just a white face, like he'd forgotten to put on the rest of his makeup.

"I heard you say something," the clown-man said. His baggy pants which puffed out at the hips were held up by suspenders. When he inched closer, it all moved like he had a giant tire around his waist.

*Don't freak out. It's just an undead clown in the Underworld.* I shivered. Maybe he was from the carnival. Then I didn't have anything to worry about. Carnival clowns are friendly, right? "Uh, nothing."

"Here. Let me help you up." He reached out, giving me a hand covered in filth. It smelled funny, too.

I pushed myself up, avoiding his hand. "My name is

Cindy," I said, introducing myself. I wasn't sure why I told him my name. Or why I was even talking to him for that matter. Birds cawed overhead. One of them shook its feathers.

Clown-man straightened his bowtie, snapping it into place. "Pleased to make your acquaintance." He reached up touching the brim of his hat. Silvery tufts of hair stuck out from under the brim like wads of stretched out cotton candy. Clown-man removed his patched-up top hat, revealing a balding head. He made a sweeping bow. "My name is D."

"D?" I questioned. "Like Dee Dee?"

"No." He laughed, a funny, yet creepy, sound. "Like *Death*. But my friends call me *Mr.* Death."

That fortune teller did tell me I'd meet death. I couldn't believe she was actually right about something!

"But I'm also the Undertaker," he added, holding up his soiled hands.

The Undertaker? "Oh!" I gasped. Bert warned that he'd rat me out. I hoped this was just a coincidence. "Did—"

Mr. Death burst out with a loud guffaw, his voice hoarse and cracking. "Yes, Bert mentioned you." He cleared his throat, snapping his bowtie again.

I knew it! That Bert wasn't to be trusted. If he'd ratted me out, what did Mr. Death know? I couldn't get my mom in trouble—and I didn't want to find out what would happen to me, either. There was no choice, I had to leave. And quick. "Well, I best be on my way." I stepped past Mr. Death, but he grabbed my skeleton arm.

"Where do you think you're going?" Dark circles appeared under his eyes.

"Umm . . . back to my casket?" I said, trying to sound convincing, though I was sure the wobble in my voice gave me away.

"Well, in that case, be my guest. Enjoy your stay in R.I.P." He bowed again, sweeping his top hat across his body. Mr. Death placed the hat back on his bald head. The circles under his eyes grew larger as he grinned. I swore razor sharp teeth were shining at me. "Oh, and Cindy?" His voice cackled like a witch.

"Y-yes?"

"Welcome . . . R.D."

"Sure. Right. R.D. That's me." I was so nervous that I felt like I would throw up. I laughed, then scurried past him and raced down the path. It felt like his eyes were on me the whole way. I kept running. I didn't care about anything except getting out of the Underworld. And fast!

I ran past grass with eyes that watched me. Flowers that suddenly didn't look so beautiful and butterflies that were definitely bats. Finally, I saw the elevator!

But the faster I ran, the further away it seemed. Panicked, worried, and wishing I'd followed the rules of R.I.P. (yeah, smarty-pants me, broke all three), I reached the elevator. All I wanted was to get home. I felt around, but there was no way to open it.

The key! Breathless, I turned it in the lock of the door. Jammed. I banged on the glass. Nothing. "C'mon. C'mon.

Open up!" I pushed the key in again, wiggled it, and like magic, the door opened. Once I stepped inside, I pressed all the buttons. I was too scared to care.

I peeked out of the glass door to see Mr. Death standing outside, glaring at me. He reached out grabbing onto the glass. But his hand slipped and he fell. He landed on the ground, scowling. "Just you wait." He shook a fist in the air.

Those words were enough for me to know it wouldn't be the last time I'd see him.

chapter 17

The next day after school, New-mother had a list waiting for me on the counter. Great. Chores. But, if it got me to the dance, then I suppose it was worth it. The note was numbered, so I knew it would be bad before I even started working.

1.  Scrub the walls in your mother's room. Use the brush in the bucket.
2.  Wash the dishes in the kitchen sink three times.
3.  Go to Mr. Occhio's store and buy a package of chicken livers. Use the change to pay the overdue fees at the library.

I tucked the note in my pocket—feeling the skeleton key—and climbed the stairs to Mom's room. I hadn't been in there since she died. It just felt too strange and sad. Dad had slept in the guest room after Mom fell ill, so it was probably weird for him, too.

When I walked in, I noticed that the furniture had been moved to the center of the room. Plastic sheets lined the floor.

## TIME OUT!

*I was offended at that. What was she trying to say, anyway? That I'd be a messy worker? How rude. It's not like I'm in kindergarten or something and have to wear a smock during art class.*

On the bathroom floor was a bucket with a brush inside. When I pulled it out, I gasped. It was mine.

New-mother must have been playing some weird, cruel joke—I couldn't clean with a hairbrush! I ran back downstairs and looked under the kitchen sink for a real scrub brush. I looked all over, but there wasn't a scrub brush to be found anywhere in the house!

I realized that if I wanted this chore done, I'd have to use my hairbrush. That seemed totally unfair.

Sulking my way back upstairs, I filled the bucket with water and started scrubbing the walls with my hairbrush. Not only did the chore seem pointless, but it took so long my arms ached.

I bet Hagatha didn't even care that I still had homework to do. Not to mention all the other chores to complete.

When I was done, I closed the door to my mom's room. A mixture of emotions crept up on me.

Anger and sadness.

Anger and frustration.

Anger, anger, anger.

I wanted to throw something, scream and kick. And pout. I wished my mom were here. It's not like she did anything special in R.I.P. As far as I could tell, she just sat down there all day sipping tea and eating crumpets. The Underworld could have taken anyone. Why did they need her? Plus, I didn't understand why my dad replaced her so quickly. And I didn't understand why New-mother insisted on making me do this list of stupid chores. She was nothing short of a monster.

And that, I decided, was a perfect name for her— Momster. Because she was part mom, but mostly monster.

I carried the bucket downstairs and put it away under the kitchen sink along with all the other cleaning supplies. That's when I saw the brushes. Brushes of all sorts. Cleaning brushes, scrubbing brushes, hair brushes. There must have been a dozen of them. They definitely weren't there when I had looked for them. Momster must have hidden them so I wouldn't have a choice but to use my own hair brush.

How horrible of her! When I stood up, I noticed all the dishes. Not only did they fill the sink, but they were spread across the counter too. And they were all clean. They didn't even need to be washed! What was wrong with that lady? I wasn't going to wash clean dishes. I tucked some of them back into the cabinets, but Momster walked in the room, clearing her throat. I nearly dropped a plate.

"Have they been washed?" she asked, tapping her foot. "Three times?"

I didn't bother answering. I just filled the sink with plenty of soap and started washing the dishes.

Momster removed the ones from the cabinet that I had put away. "Don't forget these."

"But they're already clean," I protested.

"Just. Keep. Washing."

So I did. I washed all the dishes. Once. Twice. Three times. They weren't any dirtier or any cleaner than they were to start with and I thought it was just a stupid waste of time. Frustrated, I let them drip dry, since Momster hadn't told me to dry them or put them away. Only to wash them three times.

Momster handed me some money. "For the groceries."

I took the money, shoving it deep in my pocket, right beside the skeleton key, and went to Occhio's store. The butcher watched as I paced back and forth in front of the meat counter, searching for the livers.

"Chicken livers?" he asked.

"Yeah. How'd you know?"

He chuckled. "Lucky guess." He pointed to some dark-looking meat in the glass case. "How much?"

"What?" I asked.

"How much liver you want?"

"Oh." I pulled the money from my pocket and counted. "I dunno. I've got thirteen dollars. But I need change."

"Well, then," he said bundling up a heaping portion of livers. "This ought to do you nicely." He handed me the package.

At the register, I paid for the livers. $10.75.

Then I walked to the public library, which was only a block away, the change and key jingling. Late fees were only $2.25 and that was exactly what I had left in my pocket.

For a second, I thought it was odd that Momster knew exactly how much money I would need. But I figured she just didn't trust me to return the change to her. Maybe she thought I'd keep the change and use it to buy something for myself.

When I left the library, the sky started changing colors and before long the sun would set. I knew I didn't have much time to get home before I'd turn into a skeleton. Part of me wanted to blame Momster for this. Like it was her fault I'd have to race home. But there was no way she could have known I was a skeleton at nightfall. And if she did know that, it would have been horribly mean of her to do that to me.

Momster waited at the door. "You made it back just in time."

"Sure did." I nodded confidently. "Wait. What?"

"For dinner." Momster smiled.

"Right. Dinner." I tried not to sound too frazzled.

Momster reached for the bag of chicken livers. Her eyes darted from me to the bag to the floor where a puddle of blood had collected.

"Bertha," Momster called. "Bring a towel." As soon as Bertha brought the towel, Momster wiped up the mess and handed the dirty towel to me. Then she went into the kitchen, put the livers on the counter, and started cooking.

I followed her, placing the towel on the counter. "We're not having *those* for dinner, are we?" I felt sick at the thought. My mouth filled with a burpy-urp—you know, one of those burps that has a little bit of vomit in it—and I covered my mouth to hold it back.

"We're not." Momster looked at me and smiled like the Devil (or maybe Mr. Death). "But you are."

## chapter 18

"That's not fair," Winnie said aloud. Momster shot a death-ray stare at her. "I'm really sorry," Winnie whispered to me out of the corner of her mouth as she hung her head. The way she said it, she sounded like she actually felt sorry that I'd have to eat the livers.

"Me too," Bertha mouthed from across the table.

I didn't want to look at either of them. I missed my dad's cooking and I wondered why he let this woman get away with forcing me to eat livers. Who knew what she'd make me eat next.

Winnie's eyes caught mine as I twiddled with a napkin under the table. She smiled, her teeth sticking out over her lips. "It'll get better, I promise."

What did she know about things getting better? From what I could tell, things were pretty good for her. She didn't have to eat livers. She didn't have a secret curse that turned her into a skeleton and she didn't have Death waiting for her in the Underworld. Plus, Momster treated her nicely.

Bertha reached for my hand, but I pulled away. She was acting weird and so was her sister—I didn't like it. Not one bit.

When dinner was served and everyone else got to eat tacos with fresh salsa and lettuce, I got stuck eating chicken livers and onions. But, knowing that I had only moments before the sun would set, I scarfed down my dinner—even though it almost made me barf—and raced to my room just in time. Locking the door behind me, so no one could see my transformation from Cindy into skeleton, I fiddled with the key from my mom. It needed a chain, but I couldn't find one. I grabbed a blue hair ribbon, strung it through the looped end of the key, and slipped it over my hand, letting it dangle from my wrist. Then I flopped on my bed and flipped through a magazine. A knock came at my door.

"Who's there?"

"It's me. Winnie." Her voice came softly through the door, almost like she was unsure about talking to me.

Although I still had the magazine in my hand, I wasn't really paying attention to the stuff on the pages. Instead I was thinking about my next trip to the Underworld. I had to see my mom and tell her about the stuff Momster made me eat. For sure she'd take my side and feel sorry for me.

But then I remembered my encounter with Mr. Death. How could I go to the Underworld when creepy clown-man was waiting for me? What would he do to me if I returned? Especially if he found out I wasn't really an R.D. Worse, what would he do to my mom once he learned she was responsible for it?

Hands shaking, the key clanging against my bones, I put the magazine down. "What do you want?"

"Um, well . . ."

My patience wore thin with anxiety. "Winnie, please. What is it?"

She breathed a long sigh, loud enough to be heard through the door. "I was wondering if you could help me with my math homework."

"Homework?" I laughed, even though I didn't mean to. It wasn't that I was laughing at her, but more at the thought of her seeing me as a skeleton. "It's late, Winnie. Go to bed."

Winnie didn't respond, so I ran across the room, my bones clattering the whole way. Those noisy bones would give me away! All I wanted was to press my skull to the door, and maybe do a little super-secret-spy action. But I couldn't hear anything. Maybe she had given up and gone to bed. Or maybe she was just listening on the other side of the door, too.

Under the door, light from the hallway swept in. The tips of her shoes pointed toward my room. "Winnie?" I didn't really want to sound like I cared, but I was curious to know why she was so quiet. "Winnie? You still there?"

Winnie gasped. At least it sounded like a gasp. It was the kind of sound you make when you're shocked or surprised. Or choking on something.

Then I heard Winnie's frantic footsteps echo as she ran from the hall all the way down the stairs. There wasn't anything after that. Except for me gasping as I looked down at my feet.

My skeleton feet.

Maybe she'd seen them. Oh, no! What if she did? She'd probably blab it all over school then everyone would know my secret. They'd all think I was a freak. Sarah wouldn't be my friend anymore. And Ethan would never call or leave another message. Not even one about my notebook.

I had to do something about it. Something to keep her quiet. So I schemed up a plan. It meant I'd have to miss a night with my mom, but I was sure she'd understand. Especially if she knew Mr. Death was waiting for me.

Later that night, when it was completely dark outside and I was sure Winnie and Bertha were fast asleep, I snuck into their room and stood at the foot of their beds.

## TIME OUT!

*I'm a total scary movie expert. So I knew my plan would work. This is how it goes: A person sleeps in their bed. A scary thing (that would be me) hovers next to them. Sleeping person wakes up because their brain pulls them from their dream and tells them, "Wake up stupid—there's a monster at your bedside and it's going to eat you alive." Person wakes up, realizes that it wasn't a dream, and they scream their heads off. Person = scared. Monster = justified.*

I stood there and watched and waited.

And waited.

In fact, I waited so long that an early spring storm rolled in and the sound of rain and thunder echoed in the room. But they didn't wake up.

Bertha snored. It was really loud, too. It kind of reminded me of a chainsaw. The sound drummed in my head. I had to rub my skull a few times to remove the numbing sensation.

Winnie did a lot of grumbling and mumbling, moaning and groaning, tossing and turning. I wondered what she must be dreaming about to be so restless. She would be pretty tired in the morning after all that activity.

It seemed like I stood there forever.

And that's when I decided that all that stuff in movies was fake, just to get us scared about falling asleep

I needed to do something drastic to wake them.

Since Winnie seemed like she wasn't getting much rest anyway, I thought I'd go with her first. Without really thinking it through, I grabbed her blankets and pulled them off really fast, like a magician pulling a tablecloth off a table and all the glasses and dishes stay put. But Winnie didn't budge. Just like those dishes.

With the blankets gone, she was finally still. No more grumbling and mumbling, no more moaning and groaning, and no more tossing and turning.

Bertha snored loudly and I turned toward her. Poor girl would have a sore throat in the morning. She seemed like she could sleep through anything, too deaf from the snoring. Since noise wouldn't wake her, I had to do something that she could feel. Maybe if I took her pillow away, she'd wake up from the movement.

I grabbed the pillow and tugged. Just then, a huge bolt of lightning struck. I counted the seconds before the thunder came, to see how close it was, but couldn't make it past one.

As soon as the thunder exploded, Bertha rolled over, her eyes peeking open.

Bertha looked at me, obviously not processing what she saw. But then another flash struck outside, lighting up the room and Bertha sat up in a start. Then she screamed. At. The. Top. Of. Her. Lungs.

"What's the mat— " Winnie mumbled half-asleep. She blinked her eyes. Then she looked in my direction "Ska-ska-skeleton!" Her voice was all shaky.

Bertha still screamed.

Finding it all terribly funny, I covered my mouth and laughed.

Dad came running into the room, and Momster followed behind him. He switched on the light. His eyes darted from Winnie to Bertha to me. My dad didn't say anything; he stood there with his arms folded. Then he got a look. It said, *You're in big trouble, missy, and you better get to your room because if you don't I'm going to get all kung-fu on your butt.* Yeah, I knew the look. All too well.

With my head hung low, I skulked right past Dad.

Momster didn't say anything and I figured she must have known my secret. Any normal person would freak out if they saw a real, live skeleton standing in their house in the middle of the night. Winnie and Bertha were perfect examples of that.

I went to my room and sat on my bed. My body shook with laughter as I chuckled to myself thinking about the looks on my stepsisters' faces; Winnie with eyes as big as

dinner plates and Bertha screaming with her mouth as large as a melon, and black as a cave.

The commotion coming from Winnie and Bertha's room continued. Voices carried down the hall and I heard every word. I wondered why they didn't try whispering. It was almost as if they wanted me to hear their conversation.

"Now, now girls, calm down," Momster said.

"But she's a freaking skeleton, Mother," Bertha said.

"Why didn't you tell us?" Winnie said.

"Because it's her secret," I heard Dad say. "And she doesn't like people to know."

"Seemed like she wanted us to know tonight," Winnie said.

*Yep. You got that right.*

"Why couldn't she have shown us during the day?" Bertha asked.

"Because it only happens at night," Dad said.

"Girls, enough questions," Momster said. "And you won't speak of this to anyone. What happened here, stays here. Got it?"

Silence followed after that and I figured they were nodding their heads.

"What's wrong with her?" Winnie finally asked.

"It's why we're here," Momster said.

## chapter 19

Everyone sat quietly at breakfast. Winnie and Bertha hid their faces behind cereal boxes, pretending to read them, but it was obvious they were avoiding me.

"Morning," I mumbled.

"Morning," they mumbled back.

"Cereal?" Dad asked, holding up a box of sugar-coated oats.

"Sure." I snatched it and sat at the opposite end of the table from Winnie and Bertha. Not like that was super far from them, since the table barely sat five people.

Momster walked into the room. "Good morning, Cindy."

I searched her face for "the look." When I didn't see it, I studied her face again for *any* look. But her face was blank. Pleasant, but blank.

"Did you sleep well?" she asked as she spread a napkin across her lap.

I shrugged. "I guess."

"Good." She turned to her daughters. "And you, Bertha? Winnie?"

The girls peeked around their cereal boxes, just enough so they could see Momster.

"Did you sleep well?" Momster repeated.

I watched her face and that's when I spied "the look." It said, *You better lie and say you slept great or you're both grounded.*

The girls nodded. They obviously knew Momster's looks well. Momster cleared her throat and the girls sat up straighter in their chairs.

Winnie pushed her cereal box out of the way, but her eyes remained glued to her bowl. "You walking to school with us today, Cindy?" This little skit had clearly been rehearsed, and Winnie strived to give it her best effort.

"Sure," I said, attempting to be nice only because I felt bad for scaring them last night. When we finished eating, we put our dishes in the sink, gathered our things, and walked to school. I gripped the key, still tied around my wrist, thinking of my mom. She'd be proud that I was trying. Well, okay, but I wasn't exactly *not* trying either. Winnie and Bertha didn't talk at all. Not even to each other. Once the brick building was in sight, I took off searching for Sarah. Thankfully, I didn't have to look far. She waited for me at my locker.

"So, the Spring Fling dance is tomorrow night." She pulled at my hand, bubbling over with excitement. "Can you go?"

There was no easy way to tell my best friend about Momster and the horrible chores she was making me do in exchange for a few hours at a dance.

"Aren't you excited?" Sarah asked.

"Uh, yeah. I guess."

"What's wrong?" I knew she sensed something was up because her face got that look where one eye goes all twitchy and her lips are drawn into a little pout. Since she'd read right through me if I lied, there was no choice but to tell her.

"I just have chores to do."

"Well, maybe I can help." Sarah opened her notebook like she was ready to make a list. "What kind of chores do you have to do?"

"Just stuff." I rifled through my locker, pretending to search for something. "Don't worry about it. I'll figure it out and we'll have a great time."

"And then you can dance with Ethan McCallister."

I gave her shoulder a little shove. "Maybe you can dance with his brother."

"Shut up." Her cheeks turned pink and she pushed me back, playfully.

Her embarrassment told me that I was right. She liked Ethan's older brother, Hunter. "Don't worry. I hear he likes younger girls."

Sarah stuck her tongue out, her nose crinkling. Then we both burst out laughing.

At that same moment, Ethan walked up. "Hey, Cindy." He gave a wave in mid-air.

"Hey." I tried not to blush. But I did anyway. I could feel it. Being a skeleton would have saved me from that embarrassment. No pink cheeks. Though it probably would have opened a different can of worms.

"Did you get my message?"

I nodded.

"Ms. Lilly from the front office asked me if I could take it to you. Your notebook, I mean." He placed his backpack on the floor and dug around in it. He pulled out a purple spiral pad. "Sorry I didn't get it to you sooner. I kind of hoped you'd call me back. With a good time to stop by, I mean. Ya know? Didn't want to just drop in."

That was smart thinking. I definitely wouldn't have wanted him showing up when I was a skeleton. That would have been humiliating. He'd probably go running the other way. Maybe even hitch a ride and hightail it out of town.

Ethan handed me the notebook. On the front cover was my name with a heart next to it. But underneath that— well . . . underneath that was the worst part. The words *I LOVE ETHAN* were written in big letters across the entire notebook.

My face flushed hot. I wanted to die. How could I not remember I'd written that? And where was the girls' bathroom when I needed it? "Eh. Yeah. Um, thanks." I grabbed the notebook from him and quickly shoved it in my locker.

"Sure. No problem." Ethan crossed one arm over his chest, leaning against the locker adjacent to mine. "So, if you want, I could come by this afternoon and help you catch up."

That would have been amazing. But chores waited for me, and Momster would see to it that I never had a life. "Maybe another time." There was no way I would tell him about my situation. I'd just look like the dork of the century.

"Well, if you change your mind, just give me a call."

"Sure." But I knew I wouldn't change my mind because it's not like I could make anything different. Especially when my mom had asked me to cooperate. I would do it for her, even if I hated every minute of it.

If I was lucky, I might be able to sneak out to see her tonight. Even if Mr. Death was waiting for me, it was a risk I was willing to take. If Mom was willing to let me off the hook with the whole cooperation thing, then Ethan could come over to study. "I'll definitely let you know if anything changes."

"Okay." Ethan smiled and this little spot in my chest started to tingle.

"Thanks." I smiled back. "For the notebook and stuff."

"Anytime."

Ethan flung his backpack on his shoulder and started down the hall. That was when I saw, out of the corner of my eye, Bertha and Winnie whispering, watching. Staring. Did one of them have googly eyes for Ethan, too? Before it got too awkward, Winnie put her arm around Bertha and led her to class. Bertha glanced over her shoulder as she walked away.

chapter 20

When I got home from school, Momster had a list waiting for me, just as she had the previous day. It was numbered again. I was so thrilled. Not.

1.  Scrub the floor in your mother's room, but use the toothbrush on the sink and not the brush in the bucket.
2.  Gather up all the dirty laundry and sort it into three piles: whites, lights, and darks.
3.  Take a trip to Mr. Occhio's store and purchase pickled pigs' feet, but make sure they are dated no older than last year.
4.  Pick up the dry cleaning on the way home. The change from the pigs' feet should be just enough to cover the bill.

Her lists were odd, to say the least. She was either totally obsessive-compulsive or crazy. And that's why I would just do what she asked. I really didn't want to find out which one of those things she really was.

The only way to have fun with these chores was to make a game of it, like Mary Poppins would do. Okay, lame example, but you get the idea. Plus, attitude adjustments seemed to work in the past, so why not now? Before I started, I removed my key, placing it on my dresser, and grabbed my watch so I could time myself with each task.

After scrubbing the floor in my mom's room—which made no sense at all because it wasn't even dirty—I noticed that it took me precisely sixty-eight minutes. I thought that was odd since my birth date is June eighth (6/8). I also noticed that the toothbrush was mine and I decided that I would buy a new one at Occhio's when I purchased the pigs' feet.

I raced around the house and gathered up the laundry. I sorted it like Momster asked. The time on my watch flashed twelve minutes. *Weird. That's almost how old I am,* I thought.

After catching my breath, I walked to Mr. Occhio's store and searched the shelves for pickled pigs' feet. I saw pickles of all sorts: dill pickles, hamburger pickles, kosher pickles, and even sweet relish pickles. When I saw pickled eggs, I almost puked. The shelves were full of pickles but there was no sign of pickled pigs' feet. Not in any obvious place I could see.

I moved the jar of pickled eggs to the side and to my surprise there was a jar of pickled pigs' feet. There was only one jar, so I didn't bother checking the date.

My stomach churned as I pulled the jar from the shelf and held it out in front of me. They were worse than the pickled eggs. Little piggy hooves all jarred up for some disgusting person to eat. What was next? Pickled eyeballs? That's just plain gross.

On my way to the counter, I grabbed a toothbrush too, but when I set it all down at the register, Mr. Occhio shook his head.

"Sorry, Cindy." Mr. Occhio pushed the toothbrush away. "No toothbrush for you," he said in broken English.

"Why not?"

"N'enough money for dry cleaning."

"Fine." I gave him the money and looked up suddenly. "Wait. How did you know that?"

The man smiled, his face scrunching up like a wrinkly tomato. "You go now," he said as handed me the change. Then he shooed me out the door. Puzzled, I glanced back at him only to find him still smiling. Had Momster talked to Mr. Occhio? Did she tell him not to let me buy a toothbrush? My brain felt like it would explode.

As I walked down the sidewalk, I realized I hadn't counted the money. I'd also forgotten about timing my chores because I was so distracted with gross pickled animal parts. When I got the dry cleaning, I paid better attention. The total came to $22.25, which I thought was odd because it reminded me of the date my mom died: February twenty-fifth. I had exact change, so my pockets were bare.

When I got home, Momster waited with her arms crossed. "Did you finish your chores?"

"Yep." I put the container of pickled pigs' feet on the counter. "Here you go."

Momster turned the jar, round and round. "Good work." She tapped at the date near the lid.

I sighed, remembering I hadn't checked it. "And here's the dry cleaning." Just to be sure I didn't get too close to her, I laid it on the table.

Dad stuffed a cherry pastry in his mouth. "I'll take that."

I grabbed my dad's sleeve. "Dad?" I tried to keep my voice soft so Momster wouldn't hear.

He smacked his food. "What's the matter, Cindy?" He obviously didn't get the *I'm trying to whisper* memo because his voice was really loud and rushed, his eyebrows doing that wrinkly caterpillar thing.

"Can I have some money so I can get a new toothbrush?" I asked quietly.

"What's wrong with your old one?" Dad's voice was ten times louder than necessary. He was so clueless.

Momster, who had obviously heard the entire conversation, had a look on her face. It said, *You better not spill the beans on this one or you'll find yourself locked in your bedroom for eternity.*

"Um, I lost it." I stared at my feet, rubbing the tips of my shoes against each other.

"Lost your toothbrush?" He pulled his wallet from his back pocket and handed me a five dollar bill.

Momster took it from him, crumpling the money into her palm. "It's time for dinner." She shot me a look, her eyes cutting like razors. I just stood there pouting with my arms crossed wondering why on earth I ever agreed to this cooperation thing. I'd have to talk to my mom about that. If only Mr. Death weren't waiting for me . . .

At dinner, Momster served pot roast with mashed potatoes and gravy, and peas. My mouth started to water just thinking about how good the food would taste.

### TIME OUT!

*Maybe most kids hate peas, but I happen to love them and I don't mind admitting it. I wasn't going to lie, that's for sure. My mom told me a story once about Mr.Occhio. She said he told a lie and his nose grew so long it was like a tree branch! I certainly didn't need to worry about growing a tree branch for a nose. Being a skeleton was quite enough, thank you very much.*

Momster handed a plate to Dad first, his food steaming hot. Then to Winnie who smiled so wide her big teeth showed. Bertha was next and she anxiously held out her hands for her meal. As Momster passed it to her, the aroma filled my nose.

My stomach growled and a little wad of drool dripped from the corner of my mouth. Momster handed me my plate. I took it eagerly, ready to dive in. When I looked down, I didn't see yummy pot roast or any of my favorite foods. Nope. What I saw was entirely different.

I had a heaping serving of cold, smelly pickled pigs' feet.

chapter 21

"Gross! I'm not eating that." The smell coming from the plate was enough to make me sick. It reeked of dill, chili peppers, and slime. But worse somehow. The brine juice covered the plate in a gloppy, clear-ish goo and the foot looked like something from science class. I shoved it away. If I stared at it any longer, I might've gotten sick.

Momster raised an eyebrow as she stabbed her fork in a chunk of meat. "Guess you'll go hungry then."

"Dad, seriously, do I have to eat that?" My voice was a tad whiny just like it got when I wanted my way really badly.

"Only if you want to." He glanced at Momster with a small, sympathetic plea, like he needed her permission or something, but she scowled. Dad sat up tall, and with a firm, fatherly voice said, "I mean, of course you do. Don't be so insulting to your mother."

"Why do you always take her side?" My throat got choked

up, like a sob would burst through at any minute, but I wouldn't let it. I refused to cry. Instead, I slammed my fist down on the table. The dishes and glasses rattled and Momster dropped her fork.

Winnie and Bertha looked up from their plates, their faces expressionless. I thought they would be smiling and laughing about it since they would probably find it funny that I had to eat pickled pigs' feet for dinner. But they didn't look happy about it at all.

They stared at me a moment longer, then turned to each other, exchanging crooked-eyed glances. Bertha nodded toward the food on the stove.

Winnie got up and scurried to the counter. She stopped before she reached the stove and stood with her back to us. She shrugged her shoulders, took a deep breath, and let it all out. When she turned around, the open jar of pigs' feet was tucked under her arm. Winnie plunged her hand in the briny liquid, pulled out a foot, and stuffed it in her mouth. Juice dripped from her lips. She faked a smile when I knew she really wanted to gag.

She shot a look at Bertha. It said, *You better get over here and eat one too or I'm going to make sure everyone at school knows all your juiciest secrets. Including how you have a secret crush on Ethan McCallister.*

Bertha, already finished with her dinner, looked like she couldn't eat another bite. But she pushed her chair out from the table and waddled over to Winnie. Bertha reached for the jar, stuffed her pudgy arm inside it, and pulled out a foot. She shoved the pickled animal part in her mouth.

My nose crinkled as I watched them chewing and crunching. Slurping and gagging. Dad turned green and covered his mouth with a napkin. Momster? Well, she sat back and watched with pride.

There was something about what Winnie and Bertha had done that made me feel warm and kind of happy. Not because they were eating the horrid, smelly pigs' feet. But because they didn't *have* to.

### TIME OUT!
*It almost seemed like they cared or something. But they couldn't care because if they did, then I would have to be nice to them.*

Winnie, her mouth still full of foot, waved her hand at my plate, gesturing for me to eat one. But I didn't have to eat just one. I had to eat three. And while putting one in my mouth would be hard enough, there was no way I'd be able to choke down three.

"Come on," Winnie said, chewing away. "It's not that bad."

I knew she was lying because she made that face my dad makes when he eats asparagus. Her nose wrinkled, her lip curled up in a snarl but the whole time she tried really, *really* hard to smile.

Bertha made a loud gulp, squeezing her eyes shut as she swallowed. Then she stuck out her tongue, proving she had eaten it and not hidden the foot under her tongue or in her puffy cheeks. "Done." She lumbered over to me, stuck my fork in the foot and lifted it to my mouth. "C'mon, Cindy. It's not that bad. Really."

"I bet if you plug your nose, it will help," Winnie said. "I wish I had done that."

Glancing at Winnie, I gave her a look. It said, *Gee, thanks a lot.*

"Really, you won't mind it so much if you chew really fast." Bertha waved the pig foot under my nose.

That's when my dad and Winnie started banging their fists on the table in a steady rhythm. "Cin-dy, Cin-dy, Cin-dy," they chanted together. Bertha joined in, except she didn't slap her hands on the table; she inched the fork closer to my lips.

Momster just sat and watched. And waited.

With all their chanting, I felt powerful. I closed my eyes, plugged my nose, and opened my mouth. Bertha shoved the fork in quickly and I chomped down on the pickled pig foot, juice squirting down my throat. The foot was kind of soft and crunchy, a tad spicy, and a lot salty. I kind of wished it tasted like potato chips, but there was no way that was happening because my brain would never believe it.

As I moved the half-chewed food around in my mouth, I swore I felt a hair on my tongue. I had to stop chewing for a second so my gag reflex would chill out. If it didn't, that foot would find itself spewed out all over the table. Once my heart stopped racing, I chomped up the foot, swallowing so hard it went down in one big, scratchy lump. It seemed like I could even feel it land in the pit of my stomach.

Dad leapt up from the table. "WHA-HOO!" He hooted

and hollered just like a cowboy. I almost expected him to try to rope a bull.

Winnie grabbed his hands and they danced around the kitchen. Bertha joined in and the three of them pranced—shouting, laughing, and celebrating. And it was because of me.

Still giggling, Winnie scurried over and put a hand on my shoulder. "Only two more," Winnie cheered as she pointed at my plate. She had become my biggest fan.

Bertha handed me the fork. "You can do it."

I put the fork down. My eyes watered as I saw all the smiling faces around me. For a second it almost felt like we were a family. Even Momster did an almost-smile—the corner of her mouth lifting on one side—despite her best efforts to look unhappy.

Bertha picked up the fork and handed it to me again.

I shook my head.

"C'mon," she said. "You can do it."

Instead of taking the fork, I grabbed the pig foot with my hand and shoved it into my mouth, crunching into it with my teeth.

Dad, Winnie, and Bertha all cheered, jumping up and down.

Once I swallowed it, I reached for my third and final foot. Trying not to be sick at the thought, I focused on the excitement in the room instead.

With a dramatic flair, I waved the foot in the air. Then I shoved it in my mouth.

Everyone cheered.

Even Momster.

I let out a humungous belch and collapsed back into my chair. Sweat dripped from my upper lip. It might have been disgusting, but I did it!

After dinner, Momster cleared the table and I went to my room feeling victorious. I had conquered Momster's chores and accomplished things I never thought I'd be able to do. In fact, I felt so good about myself, that when I transformed into a skeleton, I refused to stay locked in my room any longer. I opened my door and stepped out into the hall even though I knew everyone was still up.

Winnie, Bertha, Momster, and Dad all knew my secret. And although Dad didn't like me when I was a skeleton, I didn't care much. I'd grown tired of hiding from him just so he'd be happy. I needed to be happy, too.

I crept downstairs where everyone sat gathered in front of the television watching a movie and eating popcorn. There was an empty seat next to Bertha, so I sat there. I reached into the bowl and grabbed a handful of popcorn. She looked at me, and to my surprise she didn't even gasp. She just smiled.

"What are you doing up? You know you're supposed to stay in your room." Dad's voice wavered in that weird fake-sternness he'd tried once before. But I knew he was just upset.

Momster shot him a look. It said, *Shut up.* She handed me a pillow, an invitation to stay. "Nice to have you join us, Cindy."

"Thanks." I stuffed a handful of popcorn in my mouth but it just fell out below my ribcage. Winnie and Bertha chuckled, and I did too when I saw the pile of half-chewed popcorn on my lap.

Once Dad realized I was there to stay, he left the room. Momster followed him. What happened next was a whole lot of shouting.

Winnie and Bertha shot looks to each other, then at me. I shrugged. They shrugged, too. Apparently, none of us were quite sure what Momster and Dad were fighting about, but I figured maybe it had something to do with me being a skeleton.

A few minutes later, Momster returned. Without Dad. She sat on the couch and didn't say anything. When the movie ended, Momster made everyone go to bed.

Climbing the stairs to my room, I felt a wave of happiness rush over me. Had Momster stuck up for me? Had she said something that would make Dad change the way he felt?

In my room, I stood in front of the mirror. I pretended my hands were puppets again because I needed a good laugh. One hand asked, "Did you hear that ringing?" The other hand responded, "Yeah, it was just my tele-bone."

The stupid tele-bone joke made me think of Ethan's message, which made me think of the dance, which made me think of the chores I was doing, which reminded me that I'd promised Mom I'd cooperate. And all those connected thoughts made me realize that if I didn't run fast, I would miss another visit with her.

I couldn't let that happen!

Refusing to think about Mr. Death, I slipped the key around my wrist, raced out the front door, and rushed down the street to the gates of the cemetery. The black iron glistened in the moonlight and I remembered not long ago when I was afraid to go beyond the fence after dark. It was a good thing there was no dog to chase me tonight.

A howl floated through the air. *Speak of Mr. Death.*

When I reached my mom's grave, Ms. Wanda was standing there. I hadn't seen her in forever.

"Ms. Wanda! What are you doing here?"

She smiled weakly. "I was chatting with your momma, sugah."

"You were? How?"

"We have our ways." She rubbed her hand against her cheek. "I understand there's been bit of a problem down there in R.I.P."

I gulped. "There has?" If I'd been normal-Cindy my heart would have dropped to my toes.

Before she could say anything more Cheddar popped up out of the ground, the pink elevator following right after him. "Where were you? I waited all night."

"Sorry. I, uh . . . had things to do." I couldn't dream of telling him about eating pickled pigs' feet. He might think I'd try to eat his feet. Little did he know I preferred a little meat on my bones!

"Fine. But let's get going before it's too late," Cheddar demanded, crawling up my arm.

Together, we boarded the elevator. I turned to say good-bye to Ms. Wanda but she was already gone. POOF! Cheddar tolerated the ride, squished between me and the ceiling while I cheered like I was on the best roller coaster ever.

Bert was at the ticket booth which made me feel sick. Nervous, trembly, and . . . sick. "I knew it!" he said. "Good thing I already warned the Undertaker."

I gulped. I already knew Bert had told. Could that be the trouble Ms. Wanda spoke of? What would Mr. Death do to me now? My bones trembled.

"Wait here," Bert said. Then he left the ticket booth and walked to a small building with a big velvet curtain. He flung the fabric open, storming inside. A moment later, Bert emerged with Mr. Death (a.k.a. The Undertaker). They hobbled up together, Bert dragging a foot and Mr. Death's tire-shaped pants bumping Bert with each step.

"Well, well. What do we have here?" Mr. Death adjusted his bow, snapping it in place. "Another R.D?"

"No, sir. This is the one I've been telling you about," Bert said, proud of his allegiance to R.I.P.

"Oh, right, right." Mr. Death approached until he was inches from my face.

I really needed some breathing space, even though I didn't have lungs. Three feet—that's the privacy bubble. But Mr. Death obviously didn't know about that.

Mr. Death breathed heavily. His mouth smelling like decay. "Wait a minute . . . haven't we met before?"

My teeth chattered even though I tried really hard not to show I was nervous. "Uh, yes. Mr. Death, Undertaker . . . Sir."

"Right. I thought so. You're that Cindy girl, aren't you?"

"Yes, sir. That's me." I hoped Cheddar would help me out, maybe save the day, but he hid between my shoulder blades and trembled like a bag of popcorn in the microwave.

"Well, you're just the skeleton I've been meaning to speak with."

"I am?" I knew I was in trouble. A statement like that always ended in something bad. Just like when my dad said he had some great news. I really didn't want to end up like that poor goldfish.

"I tried to get you to wait on your last visit. I even shouted, 'Just you wait.' Remember?"

I gulped. That definitely wasn't good.

"When I heard that you were lying about being an R.D. I had to give you something very special."

He knew I was lying? How'd he know that? I gulped again. "You did?"

Mr. Death reached into the pocket of his raggedy pants. He pulled out one very large golden ticket with a cord attached to it. "It's a visitor's pass." He smiled as he placed the cord over my head, the ticket dangling around my neck, tickling my ribcage.

That was all? He wanted to give me a visitor's pass? "Um. Thanks?"

"When Bert told me about you, I couldn't have you

clogging the line for all the real R.D.s, so I figured this would help us all out."

"Oh." Things were definitely strange in R.I.P. "That makes perfect sense." That must have been the problem Ms. Wanda was talking about. What a relief it wasn't something else!

"Now go enjoy your stay . . . I mean, visit." He smiled, but there was something about it that looked deadly. Even though he'd given me a golden ticket and I still had a special skeleton key from my mom, I felt slightly trapped.

"Run," Cheddar commanded. "Run as fast as you can."

Not wasting a moment, I raced along the cobblestone path. Mom waited at the picket fence. She looked tired. And sad. She noticed my golden ticket and her face went pale. Mom looked scared.

"What's wrong?" A sinking feeling dropped to my toes. Maybe Mr. Death had come to visit her. Maybe she knew I'd broken the rules. Or maybe she sensed trouble like I did.

"We need to talk." Mom took my hand and led me inside.

"Okay. You need to hurry up and tell me. I'm getting kinda upset, and worried and . . ."

"Cindy, Honey," Mom said, her voice getting that tight sound. "There's something you need to know about the skeleton curse."

chapter 22

"What is it?" I asked, a panicky feeling rushing through me.

"The curse has an expiration date."

"You mean like milk?" I gulped. "Am I going to expire?" I tossed Cheddar into his basket.

Mom tried not to laugh. "Sort of." She pulled me in close and stroked my skull. "It's over. Tomorrow is our last night together."

"No! No, no, no!" I screamed. This couldn't be happening. I had just gotten used to the fact that I was a skeleton and that I could use the curse to see my mom whenever I wanted. Now it would be over, forever? "No, it's not possible." I shook my head. "Why would Dad even care then? Why would he have tried so hard to stop you? Why would he try to change me?"

"Neither of us knew that once I died the curse would eventually die too." Mom got this sad look, her face wrinkling as she tried to hold back tears. "I wanted you to visit me forever. But . . ." She shook her head. "I think maybe this is for the best. You have so many things to do and see. You can't stay here and waste your life away."

I buried my face in my mom's chest and sobbed.

### TIME OUT!

*What's it to you? So what if I cried? I was losing my mom—for a second time. I think I deserved to cry. In fact, I think I need a tissue right now.*

Mom patted my back. "I'm so sorry."

"There's no way to change it? Make it last forever?" I wiped away tears.

"I've done everything I could." Mom shook her head. "You do understand, don't you?"

Even though I didn't understand and probably never would, I nodded anyway. For her sake. I didn't want to make her feel bad because this would be hard enough on both of us. At least I had one more night. We'd have to make the most of it.

"Now let's paint some nails." Mom kissed my cheek bone, wiping away the last of my tears.

I wiggled my skeleton fingers. "Will bones do?"

We laughed together. Then I painted her fingernails and she buffed my finger bones until they shined.

After, we sat on my bed and cuddled with Scruffy. Mom made a campfire and we toasted marshmallows. But neither of us spoke much. It was too hard thinking of our next and final goodbye.

Before I left, my mom held me tight again. "One last thing," she whispered.

"Sure. What is it?"

"It's really important that you're here before nine o'clock tomorrow."

Mom had never given me instructions like that before, so it seemed a little strange. But I didn't question it. "Nine o'clock." I nodded. "No problem." I grabbed Cheddar, waved goodbye, and ran out the gate. "See you then."

At school the next day, Sarah met me at the top of the stairs. She smiled at Winnie and Bertha who had walked with me. I didn't introduce them because that was still awkward. They weren't my friends and they weren't my sisters, either.

"So, wanna go shopping after school today? My mom promised me a new pair of jeans for tonight," Sarah beamed. This dance was obviously the highlight of her year.

"Can't," I said. "Chores, remember?"

"Oh, right." Sarah glanced down at her feet, disappointed. "So what are you wearing, anyway?"

"I dunno . . ." I clutched the key's ribbon around my wrist. I had other things to worry about. Like my Mom. Like Ethan who caught my eye as he bounded up the stairs, two at a time.

"Hey, Cindy," he said, breathless.

I twirled a strand of hair around my finger. "Hi, Ethan."

"So, I was wondering . . ." He pointed to a sign on the wall announcing the Spring Fling dance. "Would you like to go to the dance?" He got that smile on his face. The one with the cute dimple. It took all my effort not to poke my finger in it. "With me, I mean."

Sarah giggled. "Of course she would."

My face flushed hotter than a pancake on a griddle. I knew I must have looked like a complete idiot. "Yeah, sure," I said, trying to make my voice as even as possible. I didn't want him to know I was excited. Regular girls might act all giggly and stuff, but I wasn't like them. At all.

"So, I'll see you tonight, then." Ethan smiled confidently.

All of a sudden, his words echoed in my head—*tonight, night, night*. It was like it just dawned on me for the very first time. "Tonight? Like after dark?"

"Yeah, that's usually what 'night' means." Ethan started to laugh, but he stopped suddenly. "So, I'll see you at the dance."

My head throbbed and I shook it to make the pain go away. "I don't know." My body felt tingly, like it floated in outer space, my head bloated and dizzy.

Sarah elbowed me in the ribs. "Of course she's going. She'll see you tonight, Ethan."

"Okay, great." He ran his fingers through his hair and turned to walk away.

"Are you okay?" Sarah put her hand on my shoulder. "You're acting funny."

I felt like I was in a trance, totally spaced out. "Tonight. Night. Night," I repeated.

Sarah laughed. "Yes, the dance is tonight, night, night." She probably thought she was being funny, but my head was too foggy to find the humor in it. "Don't you want to go? I mean Ethan McCallister just asked you!" I think she would have jumped up and down given the opportunity.

"Yeah, sure." As much as I wanted to go and dance with Ethan, I couldn't. The one thing I hadn't thought about—that was just occurring to me now—was that the Spring Fling Dance would take place after dark. And because yours truly turns into a skeleton at nightfall, there was no way I could go without everyone knowing my freaky little secret.

Then something much worse occurred to me. If I went to the dance, I would miss my last visit with my mom! "What time is the dance?"

"It starts at seven," Sarah said.

"No. I mean, what time does it end?"

"Nine. It ends at nine." She studied my face for a moment. "Why? Will you turn into a pumpkin if you stay out too late?"

I shook my head. "Not exactly." If only she knew.

My body trembled. I felt like I wanted to throw up. It was much worse than needles in my belly doing acrobatics. It was like an elephant tap dancing on my organs.

Tonight was my last chance to see my mom.

How could I possibly choose between seeing her and going to this once in a lifetime Spring Fling Dance with Ethan McCallister? Maybe I wouldn't have to choose . . . maybe there was a way I could do both.

The rest of the day at school, I was in panic mode wondering how on earth I could go to the dance without everyone finding out I was a skeleton. And trying to scheme up a way that I could be with Ethan *and* see my mom.

It was too bad it wasn't a costume party because then I could get away with wearing a sheet over my head. *Or I could just go as my skeleton self.* I'd probably get lots of compliments on how realistic my costume was.

Then that made me think of the wax museum I visited with my mom once. Those wax figures looked so real; no one could tell they were fake.

That gave me an idea.

I could cover myself in wax!

But I had no clue where I could buy a vat of wax.

The next best thing would be some modeling clay and I was sure there wasn't enough money in my pink piggy bank to pay for the cartload I'd need. The thought of my piggy bank made me sick, and I burped up a leftover taste of pickled pigs' feet.

### TIME OUT!

*I know. It's so gross. Could you imagine eating those disgusting piggy feet? Then the next day you still have that taste in your mouth. Not even Listerine could kill those germs. Yuck.*

There was no way I'd figure out how to get to the dance without being a skeleton. Even if I could find a way to hide my curse for the night and go to the dance, I'd miss out on seeing my mom.

I sighed. If only the dance ended earlier.

That was an idea! I'd leave the dance early! Then I might make it back in time and still get to visit with Mom in R.I.P!

But . . . everyone knows the end of any school event is the best part. That's when everyone goes out afterward and hangs out at the ice cream shop. I wasn't sure if I really wanted to miss out on all that fun. Plus, maybe Ethan would walk me home. If I left early that would never happen. And without finding a way to hide my curse, none of that would happen at all. No dance, no ice cream, no Ethan.

When the bell rang for dismissal, I still hadn't thought up a good solution. I pushed open the doors and clomped down the stairs where Winnie and Bertha stood.

"We waited for you," Winnie said.

"That's stating the obvious." It took tons of effort, but I didn't roll my eyes.

"I heard Ethan asked you to the dance." Bertha smiled weakly. I knew it! She did have a secret crush on him.

Winnie had this eager look on her face. "Maybe we could help you with your chores."

Bertha elbowed her in the ribs.

"What was that for?" Winnie shot a look at Bertha.

Bertha smiled a big fake smile. It was so forced that her teeth clenched together and I thought they'd shatter. I could tell she really wanted to strangle her sister.

"Oh, yeah," Winnie said shaking her head. "That's right. We can't help you."

Bertha elbowed her again.

"I mean, because Mother asked *you* to do the chores, that's why."

They were acting odd, but for them that was pretty normal. Although I usually would have tried to figure it out, I decided I had much bigger problems to solve.

# chapter 23

When we got home Winnie opened the front door, tossed her bag on the bench in the hall, and plopped on the couch. Bertha lumbered to the fridge and riffled through the contents for a snack. I went to the kitchen table and picked up the note that Momster had left for me. I threaded Mom's special key through my fingers as I read the note. It was numbered again. Lucky me.

1.  Go to your Mother's room, put your toothbrush and hairbrush in the bucket, and light the red candle on the dresser.
2.  Drop the candle into the bucket and stay there until the candle has burned out.
3.  Once the glow is gone, go to Mr. Occhio's store and buy a box of hamburger patties. You may also buy a new toothbrush and hairbrush. Use the change to buy a new pair of shoes.

4. When you get home, knock on the door three times before entering.

Today's list was a piece of cake. In fact, it was so easy I thought maybe I missed something. Maybe the note was for my stepsisters instead of me. But that didn't make any sense.

I started thinking about the list, the chores, the dance, my curse . . . That's when I started to get really upset. I couldn't believe I'd wasted all that time doing all those stupid chores. I didn't need to finish Momster's lists if I wasn't going to the dance anyway. I don't know why I didn't realize it sooner. If I had, I wouldn't have eaten pickled pigs' feet or chicken livers, that's for sure.

I stared at the key on my wrist, feeling sorry for myself.

Then, all of a sudden, like a bolt of lightning, it hit me! Ms. Wanda!

I raced out the front door.

"Where are you going?" Winnie shouted.

I ignored her as I hurried to Ms. Wanda's house. I pounded my fist on her front door.

"Ms. Wanda," I panted, gasping for air. "You've got to help me."

"What seems to be the problem, sugah?"

How could I tell her? Could I even ask for a favor as big as this? Surely as my fairy godmother she could help. She wouldn't judge me. "I need to go to the dance tonight. But I'm a, well, you know." I cleared my throat, gathering my courage. "I need you to change me. Use your wand or something."

Ms. Wanda nodded. "Aha. I see. That's quite a pre-dic-a-ment."

"So you'll help?"

"Oh, sugah." Ms. Wanda tsked. "I wouldn't be able to help you with that."

"But you're my fairy godmother. You've got to be able to do something!"

"I sure is. But there's limits. Even for fairy godmothers. I can't do nothing for ya, sugah." She shook her head. "Feel real bad 'bout it, too."

Tears welled up in my eyes. What good was a fairy godmother if she couldn't even help me get to the dance?

"Smart girl like you? I'm betting you'll figure it out," Ms. Wanda smiled. It looked like she might be hiding something.

Frustrated and hurt, I crossed the yard and barged through the front door, letting it slam behind me. The list was still on the counter. I crumpled it into my fist. Then I leaned against the counter, folded my arms, and stuck my lip out in a pout.

Dad came into the room and went straight to the fridge. "Better get busy if you want to go to the dance tonight."

"I'm not going."

He placed some deli meats and mayo on the counter. "What do you mean, 'not going'?"

"Just what I said. Not going."

Dad had a puzzled look on his face, his caterpillar eyebrows crawling across his forehead.

I couldn't believe that he wasn't getting it. "Da-ad. C'mon. You seriously don't understand?"

He shrugged.

I couldn't tell if he didn't care or if he was really that ignorant. Or maybe there was something more to his actions that I didn't know about. "If I go, everyone will know my secret."

"Ah," he said as if a light bulb had gone off in his head. "I see." Then he turned away like he wasn't even interested. "Well, you better get busy with that list."

Scratch that. It wasn't that he wasn't interested—it was that he didn't hear me. "Weren't you listening? I don't want anyone to know my secret." I stretched up on my tiptoes and whispered in his ear. "Skeleton, remember?"

"I heard you." Dad sat at the table with a stack of papers. He held a pen in one hand and a sandwich in the other. "Like I said. You better get busy." Without looking at me, he put his sandwich down, held his wrist in the air, and tapped his watch with the pen.

"Um. No. Kind of not going to do it."

Dad glanced up from his work. "Oh, yes, you are." His voice sounded like he meant business. "Look here, missy. You're going to do it and you're going to like it. If you don't want to be grounded for the rest of your life, you better hop to it. Now!"

I don't need to explain the look on Dad's face because for the first time he actually said the words that showed his feelings.

With a huge, dramatic eye roll, I turned away.

"Don't give me those eyes," Dad said. "I worked hard to . . ." But he didn't finish his sentence. It was like he stopped himself before he said something he'd regret.

I opened my mouth to ask him what he meant to say, but Momster slithered into the room. Since I didn't want her to be part of the conversation, I clamped my mouth shut tight.

"Now, Cindy," she said with that fake-sweet voice grownups use when they talk to two-year-olds. "We had a deal. You do the chores and I'll make it so you can go to the dance."

"But I don't want to go anymore." I turned my back to her.

Momster walked over and knelt down on the ground in front of me. She took my hands in hers. I wanted to yank away. But when I pulled back, for the first time, I noticed a little glimmer in her eye.

Just like Mom.

"Are you sure you don't want to go?"

I shrugged, keeping my eyes focused on Mom's key as I rolled the shank against my palm. "Of course I *want* to go." It was hard not to get all teary-eyed at the thought of choosing the dance over my mom. It was even harder to accept that going to the dance would mean everyone would know my secret. "It's just—"

"That everyone will know about your skeleton curse," Momster said, finishing my thought for me. "And you feel bad because you actually want to choose the dance over seeing your mother again."

It was like she'd read my mind! She seemed to completely

understand me. Unlike my dad. "Yeah, exactly. Wait a minute." She knew about Mom and our visits? My throat went tight. "How'd you know?" I glanced up at Momster through tear-filled eyes.

"Um-hum," Momster hummed without opening her mouth. "Well, if you want to go to the dance, you should finish your chores. And I'll keep my promise and let you go." Then she turned to me and smiled. Not one of those fake smiles grownups get, either. It was a sweet smile.

Like my mom's. Which made me think how much I'd miss her. Could I really go to the dance and miss out on the last chance to visit with my mom?

"Don't worry about your mom, Cindy. I have a feeling she'll understand."

Momster acted super nice and understanding—I couldn't figure what had gotten into her. Maybe she wasn't as bad as I thought. Maybe the person with the horrible attitude was me all along.

Although it seemed pointless to do the chores, I went upstairs. I mean, unless Momster had magical powers, there was no way she could change things for me. Not even for one night.

But that glimmer in her eye . . . that smile on her face . . .

Nah. It couldn't be. She couldn't be made of magic, too. Or could she?

With a bit of hopeful anticipation, I raced into my mom's room with the list in my hand. I put my toothbrush and hairbrush in the bucket, lit the candle, and dropped it in.

The smell of cinnamon filled the air and reminded me of my mom.

I sat on the floor and thought about her while I waited for the candle to burn out. I remembered all the things we had done together. Not just the recent things we'd done in R.I.P. either. It was stuff we'd always done. Every memory was so fresh and crisp in my mind it seemed like they were happening at that moment.

There were all the silly rap songs about Dad's caterpillar eyebrows and his asparagus-eating face. All the scary movies we watched while eating popcorn and all the times she told me she loved me. The memory of the day before she got sick flashed, too. We had hamburgers on the grill and s'mores at the campfire. Her hands were so soft when she tucked me in, and her perfume smelled sweet when she kissed me goodnight.

I saw the bad stuff, too. Like when I was three and poured paint all over the carpet. Or when I was ten and Mom let me borrow her favorite necklace and I broke it. And the sad things, like Scruffy dying and Mom's funeral. But none of it seemed so awful anymore because I had all those happy memories to go with it. It was that thing my mom called it. Bittersweet.

Even though Mom wasn't here, my memories still were. And I realized for the first time that being dead didn't mean being gone. Not really. Because maybe that was what death was. Just a moving on of sorts.

I also understood why Mom had cursed me. It wasn't

just so we could see each other again. She wanted me to see she was okay. It was her way of reminding me that she was always there. No matter what.

And she knew, just like every parent does, that I *needed* that.

A change had come over me. It felt like all the bad stuff washed away, floating somewhere unseen. Now that the bad stuff was gone, I was filled with hope.

Eleven minutes and thirty-four seconds' worth of memories later, the candle burned out. I didn't bother taking the bucket downstairs. I just let it sit there on the floor with the waxy candle remains sticking all over the brushes.

As I headed out the door, Momster stopped me.

"Here's the money," she said placing some neatly folded bills in the palm of my hand. She curled my fingers around it and smiled. She did an awful lot of smiling lately. Normally, that would have weirded me out, but it didn't. I felt different somehow.

"Thanks." I studied her face, trying not to be suspicious of her recent attitude adjustment.

At Occhio's store, Imma's Real Boy, I stood in the bath and beauty section a long time. Since Momster allowed me to buy a new toothbrush and hairbrush, I splurged on the nicest ones I could find. I chose them both in a pretty blue color.

I went to the meat counter and bought cheap hamburger patties.

On the way home, I stopped at the shoe store and bought

the shoes I had seen in a magazine. Powder blue Converse sneakers without laces. They would go perfectly with a cute skirt I'd gotten for my last birthday.

I started to feel really excited about the dance and Ethan. About everything.

To my surprise, when I paid for the sneakers, I had plenty of change. I stuffed it in my pocket and, for the first time, I realized they weren't empty. And maybe I wasn't either. Maybe there was more to me than my mom being gone and my secret skeleton curse. Maybe, just maybe, there was something more to everything.

Even Momster.

# chapter 24

I skipped home, smiling the whole way. When I got to the front door, I reached for the handle, but stopped remembering Momster's instructions. So I knocked three times.

Through the door I heard Winnie and Bertha running around, their loud voices carrying all the way outside. From the sounds of it, they were fighting over who would get to answer the door. They opened it together and smiled. "Hi, Cindy," they said.

Even though I'd always thought they were awful, somehow they seemed different now. Winnie's overbite didn't look so horrible anymore, and Bertha's acne had cleared up. In fact, I'd almost say my new stepsisters were pretty.

"Can I come in, or do I have to wait?" I asked.

Momster came up behind the girls, still smiling like she had been before I left. She reached for the bag of hamburger patties. "Good to see you're back. You're just in time."

"For what?" I said. "More pigs' feet? Or how about chicken livers?"

**TIME OUT!**

*Okay, fine. Maybe that wasn't the nicest thing to say. I'm not perfect, you know. And she had made me eat some horrible stuff. That's not so easy to get over. Just because I felt better didn't mean I had forgotten every rotten thing she'd done.*

"Hamburgers," she said.

I couldn't believe my ears. She would let me eat normal food with them? I wouldn't have to eat some horrible, disgusting animal part? Just hamburger? Wow. It definitely wasn't just me who'd changed. She really was different today.

Dad carried the burgers outside and placed them on the grill. It was the first time he'd used it since last summer. The memory of that day would stick in my mind forever as the last good day before Mom got sick. I think Dad remembered that day too because he had this happy-sad look on his face, his eyebrows squeezing together, his mouth drawn into a painful half-smile.

"You all right?" Winnie asked, putting her hand on my shoulder.

Momster wrapped her arms around my dad and snuggled into his shoulder. He hugged her back. "Just fine," I answered, watching them. It was the first time I'd really seen them together, like a real couple.

When the burgers were ready, we sat at the patio table. Momster served potato salad and a watermelon that wasn't quite ripe. Dad passed around the burgers and I ate two. He looked happier than I'd seen him in a long time. "It's almost time for the dance," he said. "Better get ready."

"But . . . I can't . . ." Despite Momster's good intentions, there wasn't any way for me to go to the dance because I would still be a skeleton.

"Sure you can," said Bertha.

I shook my head. They didn't understand. How could they?

"You can go." Momster stroked my hair softly, just like Mom used to. "You upheld your end of the deal and I will too."

"I know I'm allowed to go, but my curse . . ." Before I could finish my thought the sight of the sun setting in the distance distracted me. It was too late. It couldn't be stopped now. Tensing up, I watched and waited. My body would transform any second. I closed my eyes and listened for their gasps. "I'm sorry. I know it's weird." My body tingled. When I was sure that the transformation was over, I opened my eyes and looked around at everyone. They were smiling ear to ear. "What's wrong? Why is everyone so happy?"

Dad pointed with a gleam in his eye. "Look!" He beamed.

I glanced at my hands. They were normal! I pulled back my sleeves. My arms were normal, too.

I was still Cindy!

Normal, average, middle-school Cindy.

Just to make sure I wasn't seeing things, I pinched my skin. "Ouch!"

Dad and Momster chuckled.

"W-w-what happened?"

"It was all her." Dad gestured toward Momster. "Her spell worked."

"What spell?" I'd never seen Momster perform a spell. But that twinkle in her eye, that smile, they were just like Mom's.

Just like magic.

"The chores," Winnie said. "They were part of the spell. A special spell to reverse the skeleton curse."

"She's right," Momster added.

I wanted lots of answers. "But, how—"

Momster cut me off, shooing me inside. "You're going to be late! Now, go get ready."

Winnie and Bertha tugged me by the arm, dragging me up the stairs.

Bertha grabbed a curling iron from under my sink. "I'll do your hair."

"And I'll do some makeup. You like pink, right?" Winnie held out three lipsticks; Bubble Gum Galore, Real Raspberry, and Cherry Cordial. I really didn't want anything cherry-flavored—especially if it were Chapstick. That would have reminded me of when I accidentally gave Ethan a bloody nose. Talk about embarrassing.

"That one," I said pointing to the raspberry color.

She painted some other makeup on me too, but I couldn't see because she made me close my eyes. When Winnie and Bertha were done, they stepped back.

"You look beautiful." Bertha handed me a mirror.

Smiling at my reflection, I thought about how things had changed. I put the mirror down and picked up a rosy-colored blush and swept it across Bertha's cheeks. "Thanks. So do you."

"Hurry up, girls," Momster called. "You're late!"

As Winnie and Bertha headed out my bedroom door, I squeezed the key in my palm, my heart full. I called after them, "Wait up!"

We raced downstairs, giggling and laughing—just like real sisters.

"You only have until nine o'clock." Momster clipped a sparkly flower-shaped barrette in my hair. "Then the spell will be broken."

Dad's smile dropped like an atomic bomb in the middle of the floor. KA-BOOM! "You mean it's not permanent?"

"No," Momster exhaled, holding back a pained expression. "It's only temporary."

Dad's face grew pale. It turned a shade of white I'd never seen before, like sour milk but worse. "Why? How can that be?"

"Because it doesn't need to be any other way." Momster's eyes were full of an understanding that my dad didn't have.

"But, I thought we agreed—" Dad said, his voice ten octaves higher than usual.

"No." Momster shook her head and one eyebrow went up super high. That wasn't good. "We agreed that I'd reverse the curse. I never said it would be permanent."

Dad's chin nearly dropped to the floor.

"Thanks." For the first time ever, I hugged Momster. My face scrunched up when I looked at Dad. I refused to cry. He would never understand me. "But no one needs to worry about that. The last time I visited Mom, she said the curse would expire, so I'll be back to normal tomorrow. You don't have to worry about my hideous skeleton curse ever again."

"That's not what I—" Dad started to say.

"It's okay. You don't have to explain." I folded my arms across my chest. "I get it."

Momster's face grew weary as she exchanged glances with my dad. I wasn't sure exactly what it was they were trying to say to each other, but I knew something wasn't quite right.

Dad gave a big shoulder-shrugging sigh. "You better get to the dance before it's too late." The curses and spells, changes and un-changes, must have been too much for him because he fell into a chair with a pathetic moan. He had a long road ahead learning to accept me the way I was.

"Go on. Just remember," Momster tapped her watch. "Nine o'clock."

"Nine o'clock." I put my finger to my head like I locked it in my memory. "Got it."

chapter 25

All the hair curling and makeup applying made us late. Winnie and Bertha linked their arms with mine and we skipped to school together, giggling the whole way. Even though I had a lot of fun as a skeleton, it felt good to be normal, middle-schooler Cindy. It meant I could be outside after dark with other people, doing things that other middle-schoolers would do. My face hurt from smiling so much.

When we arrived at the dance, there were tons of kids. But they were mostly in one spot. The bleachers. The dance floor was empty. Figured. Guess I was the only one who liked dancing to "Staying Alive."

I glanced around the gym, hoping to see Ethan. Maybe he'd changed his mind about wanting to go to the dance with me.

That's when I noticed the whole place looked like a rainbow vomited. There were huge balloons everywhere in shades of neon pink, green, and blue.

Not only did the balloons plaster the ceiling of the gym, but there was also a big arch covered in more balloons. Behind the arch was a cartoon-like backdrop of a meadow. A guy snapped pictures of couples posing in front of it. A group of girls who looked like they didn't have dates linked arms and pushed their way through the crowd, cutting the line. When they reached the photographer they made funny faces for their picture.

Absorbed in watching people being photographed, I barely heard Sarah behind me.

"Cindy, Cindy!" Sarah said. "You made it! I thought you'd never get here."

"Yeah, tell me about it." If she only knew what I had to go through in order to get to the dance.

"But I thought you had chores?"

"I did." Taking her hand, I pulled her into the line to get our picture taken. "But I finished them."

"I'm so glad."

"Yeah, I am too." I was sure she had no idea just how happy I was.

"It would have been lame without you here." She glanced down at my sneakers. "Great shoes."

"Thanks." I beamed. But it wasn't just for the sneaker compliment. I was glad that my best friend thought I was cool.

Sarah leaned closer. "You-know-who was looking for you."

My cheeks burned like they were on fire. "He was?" I felt so relieved. And mortified at the same time. I'd never

danced with a boy before. What would he think of my funky chicken dance?

"He said he had to go do something, but he'd be back soon."

"Oh." I made a lame attempt trying not to sound disappointed.

The photographer called us up, snapping his fingers like he was in a hurry. We stood in front of the cheesy-looking backdrop. I made a face, sticking out my tongue, and Sarah pulled on her ears, puffing out her cheeks like a squirrel.

"Another original," the photographer said, rolling his eyes. He handed Sarah a slip of paper. "This is the link where you can download your pictures. Password is *Spring Fling.*"

"How original." Sarah rolled her eyes in imitation as she handed me the paper.

I stuffed it in my pocket.

"No one's dancing. So lame. Want to go to the cafeteria? We can get some pizza. Maybe a soda. Or they've got games in the music room. I think they're having a ping pong competition."

"Sounds great." My heart pounded, worrying that the night was going too quickly. I turned and looked at the clock. Even though it felt like we'd waited an eternity to get our pictures taken, only a half hour had passed. Then remembering that Winnie and Bertha were all alone, I stopped. "I have to do something first."

Winnie and Bertha were standing near the front entrance,

just as they were when I left them, ignored by everyone else. They were hardly even talking to each other. They looked relieved to see me.

"C'mon," I said. "Sarah and I are going to the music room. You up for a ping pong match?"

They smiled big and I could tell they were really glad I included them. All this time, I hadn't realized they might have felt just as alone as I did. Being the new kids in school must have been pretty hard for them.

There were only a few people hanging out in the game room. So there wasn't a line for ping pong. Sarah handed me a paddle. "Us against them."

"Sure." I shrugged and asked my stepsisters, "You game?"

"Okay." Winnie reached for two paddles. She handed one to Bertha while Sarah and I went to the other end of the table. We played a few games and then decided to go back to the dance.

As we walked into the gym, I felt someone tap my shoulder. I whirled around.

"Hi, Cindy," Ethan said smiling, the little dimple in his cheek making me smile back.

His brown hair stood in messy waves on top of his head. And forget about his eyes. I could hardly look at them. They made this little thing go off in my chest, and I had to suck in air.

Winnie, Bertha, and Sarah giggled, but, in true friend form, they started to sneak away.

Traitors.

"Don't-you-dare-leave-me-alone-because-if-you-do-I'm-going-to-totally-freak-out-and-die." Talking through teeth while trying to smile wasn't as easy as it seemed, and it came out as one jumbled mess.

"What?" Sarah said, a smirk building on her face. "What did you say, Cindy?" She had a tone in her voice that told me she knew *exactly* what I had said.

"Never mind." I tried to sound calm, but there was no hiding the quiver in my voice.

"I was looking for you." Ethan ran a hand through his hair and leaned against the wall.

My throat tightened. So hard to breathe. "You were?"

Ethan nodded. "Want to dance?" He held out his hand.

A bubble formed in my throat. "Sure." I didn't want to smile too big because I was afraid I'd look stupid. So I did a half-smile thing and put my hand in his.

Ethan half-smiled back. Then we walked, hand in hand, into the middle of the gym floor and danced. It kind of felt like no one else was around. Even the loud drumming of the music seemed like it was far away.

A pool of sweat had gathered between our palms, but I didn't mind. I don't think he had much of a problem with it either since he didn't look grossed out. He didn't even attempt to wipe the sweat on his jeans!

As we swayed in place, I saw Sarah dancing with Hunter and I just about freaked out for her. She smiled at me, her eyes filled with excitement. Then I noticed Winnie and Bertha waving at me from across the room.

I waved back. They must have been happy for me. And I thought it was nice of Bertha to be happy even though I was dancing with the boy she liked. Winnie pointed to her wrist. She must have wanted me to see her bracelet or something, but I figured it could wait, so I mouthed, "Later." She shook her head and pointed at her wrist again.

That's when I realized she wanted me to look at my wrist! So I lifted my arm. Maybe there was a humongous gross spider on me or something and she wanted me to swat it away before it bit me with its radioactive fangs. That's all I needed. Skeleton-Cindy to Superpower-Cindy. My life would never be normal!

But when I looked at my arm, I only saw the key from my mom.

When I glanced back up at Winnie, she pointed at the wall behind me. I turned around, but through the crowd and the rainbow of balloons, I couldn't see anything.

Ethan spun me in a circle. I almost felt like the real Cinderella. But I was glad he was dancing with me, average, middle-schooler Cindy. And not Cinderskella.

My face flushed super hot. But I couldn't worry about my face being bright red or anything because Winnie still desperately tried to get my attention. I struggled to see over Ethan's shoulder.

### TIME OUT!

*Don't say it. I already know. It's not hard to figure out. But I was so absorbed in Ethan McCallister that I couldn't think straight. You wouldn't have been able to think either. Believe me.*

She pointed again and this time, a group of kids jumped up and grabbed at a bunch of the balloons. A cloud of neon floated out of the way and I saw exactly what Winnie had been trying to show me.

A clock.

# chapter 26

I t wasn't the clock that was so interesting. It was the time on the clock. Eight fifty-seven. How did the time go so fast? Between the photos and all the ping pong games, I'd used up all my time.

My heart pounded in my chest.

There were only three minutes before my spell would break and I'd transform into a skeleton in front of everyone. Including Ethan McCallister and my BFF Sarah.

Panic? Nah. That would have been twenty minutes ago.

Fear? Nope. That would have been ten minutes ago.

Sheer terror? Yep. That was it.

I stepped away, leaving Ethan to dance by himself. It was like everything moved in slow motion. People around me seemed like they were underwater, every movement exaggerated and drawn out in these big, lengthy gestures.

Although my brain screamed, *Truck it home, girl!* My feet said, *We're stuck!* I stood there, frozen in place.

Ethan said something but it sounded like, "W – u –z – r – o – n – g."

My heart jumped and thumped around in my chest like a crazy kangaroo on an energy drink. I blinked and pulled away. "Ethan," I said, my tongue feeling like it had just bench-pressed a gazillion pounds. "I have to go."

"But . . ." He looked hurt. Or confused. Maybe both. "Don't you want to finish the dance?"

My eyes were glued on the clock. Eight fifty-nine. I couldn't stay and talk this through with him. "No. I mean, yes . . ." My head felt like it would explode. "I'm sorry." Time ticked by. Only forty-five seconds before the spell would break and everyone would know I was a skeleton. I looked at Winnie and Bertha who were standing by the door, waving for me to hurry.

Ethan reached for my hand. Forty seconds. "Please stay."

Thirty-five seconds. "I can't." I broke free and ran out the front door, following after Winnie and Bertha who were just a few steps ahead of me.

Together, we ran down the concrete stairs of the entrance. Nearly at the sidewalk, not paying attention to my footing, I tripped over a large rock right in the middle of the stair. I leapt up, despite the burning sensation on my skinned-up knees. But when I did, the movement caused the rock to wobble. The rock tumbled in a free fall down the step and fell on top of my foot. My foot was wedged tight.

"Oh, no! No, no, no. I can't get stuck. This can't happen to me!" I glanced at the doors of the school, hoping they'd stay closed. I was sure Sarah and Ethan would come flooding out of the school any second.

Winnie must have heard me because she stopped running and looked back. "I'll help." She scrambled up the steps.

"No." I shooed her away. "Go home and get help."

"Let me try first." She pushed the rock, but it didn't budge. "Sisters help each other out."

She was right. We were family. But I also knew that Winnie and Bertha didn't have any other friends. They didn't talk to anyone at school except each other. So if anyone saw them helping a skeleton, everyone would figure out the skeleton was me. "No. It's okay." I hugged her quickly, ignoring the great big tears that were ready to escape from my eyes.

"Let me give it one more try." Winnie pulled at my foot but it was still stuck.

Bertha, seeing me and Winnie struggle, hurried up the stairs. "I'll lift," she said putting her hands under my arms. "You pull."

"If you want to help me, go home." I shrugged out of her hands. If I had to chase them away, I would. "Once I transform into a skeleton it's all over." I pushed their helping hands away. "When they see you with me, they'll figure it out. They'll know that I'm a skeleton. But if you're gone, they won't know a thing."

Winnie gave me a hard look, thinking it over. "You're right." Her eyes flooded. "I'll always keep your secret." She grabbed Bertha's hand and ran.

As soon as they were out of sight, I watched as my body changed from Cindy to skeleton. My arms were skinny bones. My head became a skull and my whole body was a skeleton.

I was Cinderskella.

There was a lot of noise behind me and I turned, eyeing the door. The dance had ended and soon all the other kids would come swarming out of the building and down the stairs. Everyone would see me and then they'd know my secret. I couldn't risk that.

I had to hurry.

I pushed the rock with my hands but it wouldn't budge. Without a good grip, the rock only slipped again and fell hard against my foot, jamming it further.

Voices approached and I knew it was only moments before someone would find me.

There was no way out.

Despite my most desperate attempts to wiggle and slide my foot out from under the rock, it only got stuck worse.

Footsteps approached.

Sheer terror? Nope. That was long gone.

Death by humiliation? Yep. That was it.

Complete desperation took over and I gave a hard kick with my other foot. The stone wobbled. I let out a happy squeal then quickly kicked again. The stone wobbled some more and I saw a little piece of my blue sneaker. I slipped my hand in the opening and tried to lift the rock. But it was impossible to get a good grip and instead of making any progress, my hand became lodged in that little space like a boat inside a bottle.

No! If I didn't get out soon, everyone would know me as freaky-cursed-skeleton-girl! I'd be the laughing stock of the school.

As it was, I already looked like I was in the middle of a pathetic game of Twister. There was no option. I had to use my other hand to lift the rock. I budged the rock, the key on my wrist clanging against it. A small gap appeared and I wiggled my stuck hand, trying to free all those boney fingers as quickly as possible. But I wasn't strong enough and the rock gave way. It dropped with a crack and a snap. Fortunately, I was able to pull my hand out in the nick of time. Most of my fingers escaped . . . all of them except my thumb.

I let out another squeal because the pain came like three hundred million jolts of electricity in the form of lightning. It hurt like crazy, but I had a feeling it would have been a lot worse with skin.

There wasn't time to think about pain. I might have freed my hand, but my foot was still stuck. The bonus? The voices and footsteps were right by the door. Yeah, some bonus.

Desperate and angry, I kicked at the rock. Little pieces chipped from it, scattering on the ground. I kicked again and the rock moved, sliding so an opening between it and the concrete step appeared. And by opening, I mean a hole the size of golf ball. Hardly big enough for my foot to pass through, but it was worth a shot. With every ounce of energy in my little, boney body, I gave one last hard pull.

I did it! I finally broke free.

Unfortunately, that's literally what happened.

My foot broke off!

Yep. It was still stuck in my sneaker, lodged under the rock. I knew that blasted opening wasn't big enough.

I had two choices. A) I could make a run for it and live without a foot. Or B) I could try to get my broken-off foot out from under the rock. Even though I might be able to live without a foot, I knew people would figure it out if they ever found my sneaker. Or saw my footless leg . . .

Decision made. I needed my foot.

So, trying to ignore the pain, I attempted to lift the rock again. It moved just enough that the golf ball-sized opening became as large as a tennis ball. Great. Still, it was better than nothing. As I grabbed my foot-filled sneaker, I looked up to see Ethan walking down the stairs.

## chapter 27

Time was up. So I left my sneaker and foot behind and RAN! Actually, I hobbled, all the way home. I hoped I did it before anyone could see me, but I wouldn't really know because I never looked back. I was too afraid.

Pain throbbed in my ankle where my foot used to be and I fought hard not to cry. I wasn't sure what was worse: the pain, or knowing I didn't have a foot anymore.

When I reached the front door, it was wide open and I saw Winnie and Bertha bent over their knees, wheezing for air.

"Cindy," Bertha gasped.

"Stuck," Winnie said, panting.

"Home," I said, my bones clunking.

Winnie and Bertha turned around and when they saw me, their eyes welled up with tears. They ran over to hug me.

"How'd you get out?" Winnie asked.

"A small sacrifice." I held my broken thumb in the air.

"And a little bigger of a sacrifice." I lifted up my footless leg. Normally I'm not a good faker, but since I was a skeleton I didn't even have to try to hide the pain on my face.

"I'm so sorry," Momster said, rushing to my side. "I knew I should have never—"

"No." Dad set his eyes on Momster. "I should never have let you." He walked over and knelt at my side. "Oh, Lovie. I'm so sorry." He lifted me up, hugging me. He cradled me in his arms and carried me to the couch. It was the first time in my skeleton form my dad had hugged me. And I noticed that he didn't look sick the way he used to. Maybe he was finally getting used to me being a skeleton.

"Does it hurt much?" Momster asked.

I shook my head, trying to be strong.

She held out her hand. "Give me the thumb. I'll snap it back in."

I handed it to her and covered my face as she popped it in place. I wiggled my fingers and thumb. It didn't hurt. Much.

"You need to see a doctor," Dad said.

"No doctor." I tried to give him a look, but because I was a skeleton nothing changed. Still, I thought, *This story is so unbelievable that if you told anyone about it they'd think you needed to see a doctor.*

Momster read my mind and said, "How would we explain it?"

"I don't know." Dad scratched his forehead, his arm, then his face. He scrunched his eyebrows together until

they made one great big wiggly line in the middle of his forehead. "But we need to do something about Cindy's foot."

Winnie put her hand to her forehead, mocking a salute. "We won't let a good man down, will we, soldier?" She directed her efforts at Bertha in her best drill sergeant voice. "We're going back there. And we'll find your foot."

Momster tearfully hugged her daughters. "I'm going, too."

As soon as they were out the door, Dad held me tight. "I'm sorry, Lovie." He stroked my bald skull.

"It's okay," I said, trying really hard to be strong. It was a different strong than when my mom died. It was an *I can bear this* strong. Not an *I'll never get through this* strong. Because never getting through something wasn't really strong at all.

Dad started shaking all over, his body trembling like it was its own earthquake. "This is all my fault."

"What do you mean?"

"I didn't want you to be a skeleton. I hated it. I was angry with your mother for what she'd done. All I wanted was for you to be yourself again."

My dad started crying and it seemed weird. Even when my mom died, he never cried in front of me. He'd broken down with Pastor Stan, but he didn't know I was watching. During those dark days, he had held it together for me. Maybe now he felt it was okay to cry because I was strong enough to bear it.

"But I was happy."

Dad nodded. "I know that now. That's why this is my fault. If I hadn't insisted Hagatha change you, you'd still have your foot," my dad said between sobs. I'd never seen him fall apart like this.

"It'll be okay." I patted his back, comforting him, even though my ankle throbbed and I was the one that could use some pampering. "I'll be just fine, even if I never have my foot back."

"I wish I could have seen that you were happy being Cindy-skeleton all along."

I corrected him. "It's Cinderskella."

"Oh." He smiled, wiping away tears.

"It took a while. But I got used to being different. Even if I don't want people to know."

Dad hung his head. "If I had been more accepting, you would have been too." He pulled me tight and kissed the top of my skull.

"It helped that I got to visit with Mom." I missed her so much right now. She always knew what to do and how to make me feel better. Then I sat up like a bolt. "Wait . . . I'm still a skeleton . . . that means I can visit her!" Her curse didn't expire like she said it would.

Dad's eyes got big. Not as big as they did the first few times I turned into a skeleton, but close. "I guess so."

"I thought her spell would expire. I mean, that's what she told me during our last visit." My bones rattled with excitement as I found the energy to leap off the couch. Suddenly, I understood everything. The curse. Momster. The lie. The

reverse curse. Mom wanted me to be happy, and she realized I was strong without her. That I was okay. That's why
she lied about the spell expiring. That's probably what she
meant when she said it was for the best. "I'm going to see
her right now."

"I'll go with you."

If I could have given a look it would have said, *And how
on earth do you expect to get into R.I.P?*

I thought about grabbing Mr. Death's golden ticket from
my dresser, but I didn't need it. I clutched the key in my
palm. "To the cemetery."

"Let's go." Dad picked me up, my bones clunking against
him.

I nodded. And even though Dad couldn't see it, I smiled.

He carried me to the black gates of the cemetery and
swung them open. Then he trudged through the graveyard straight to Mom's headstone. Dad lowered me to the
ground. The elevator stood majestic as always with its colorful, flashing lights, beckoning me to board it. But I didn't.

Cheddar scampered out from behind the elevator.
"You're late," he said. "Your mother told you to be here by
nine and you missed it. It's all over. I got nothing for you.
Zip. Zilch. Nada."

"Magic never dies. It lives on in each of us. That's how
I knew the spell wasn't really going to expire," I said. "She
just told me that. She knew about the dance and wanted
me to go and have fun. And Momster helped her. Momster
helped all along."

Cheddar tipped his head and twitched his tail. "You humans are all the same. You think you got all the answers."

"But I'm right. And you know it."

"Fine. But I'm not taking you down there. My job here is done. Thank you very much."

Dad leaned over and whispered to me. "Is he always this cranky? Don't tell me Mom made you put up with him all this time."

I nodded. "Every night." I glanced at Cheddar. "Don't worry. I don't need to see her."

Cheddar's little skeleton jaw nearly dropped to the ground.

Dad's mouth opened in shock, too. "You don't?"

"Nope." My fingers curled around the key. I had everything I needed. The gift she'd given me was enough. Mom knew I'd figure it out. Being myself was the key.

"Then why are we here?" Dad asked, puzzled.

"Yeah. What are you wasting my time for?" Cheddar flipped his tail in the air.

I looked at Dad. "You got a pen and paper?"

He reached into his shirt pocket and pulled out a pen and a small notepad. "How's this?"

"Perfect." I took it from him and scribbled a note.

*Dear Mom,*

*I understand what you did tonight. I know that you and Momster were working together to help me. I figured it all out. And I love you for it. It was the hardest decision I ever had to make, but I know you did it to help me. I'll miss seeing you, but I know that I need to have fun still. In the real world. With real friends. Who aren't dead. But that doesn't mean I'll ever forget you. Because I'll be back once a year. On your birthday. Just so you don't get lonely.* ☺

*XOXO*
*Cinderskella*

I rolled up the note and handed it to Cheddar.

"I'll make sure that she gets this." Cheddar slipped the note between his ribs. Even though he was a skeleton mouse and he couldn't smile, I knew he did. Because I skeleton-smiled, too.

I put my hand against the glass, proud of my decision. Proud of who I was—skeleton curse and all.

## chapter 28

As we walked away, I swore I heard carnival music playing softly in the distance. There was a sound of tinkling glass, too. But I didn't look back. I didn't need to.

When we got home and were seated comfortably on the couch, Winnie, Bertha, and Momster dragged themselves through the front door.

"I'm sorry, Cindy. I tried," Winnie said. "We all did."

"But it was already gone," Bertha blurted out.

"Bertha! You weren't supposed to tell her that." Winnie did her best to hide her emotion behind gritted teeth.

"What do you mean it was already gone?" I felt panic rise up from my not-really-there belly.

"Quiet now, girls," Momster said. "We'll find it in the morning." She walked over and kissed the top of my skull. "It's bound to show up."

"Thank you," I whispered to her. "For the spell and trying to help me. But, how did you know?"

"Your mom was my best friend."

So Mom wasn't siding with a horrible stranger all along! She was trying to help her best friend—and her daughter.

"We made promises to each other a very long time ago. And I'd do anything to help her little girl." Her eyes twinkled just like Mom's and I knew that the three of us shared something very special.

Magic.

Dad smiled proudly. "I think I'll get a snack ready." Dad walked into the kitchen.

"I'll help." Momster followed behind him.

As they walked away I had a feeling if I didn't have my foot tonight, I might never get it back.

A moment later, Dad and Hagatha brought in a tray of snacks and set it on the coffee table. As we munched on pretzels, a knock came at the door. Dad went to answer it and held the door open wide.

Ethan McCallister walked in. I ducked behind the couch as fast as I could. I couldn't believe my dad had let Ethan into the house while I was a skeleton!

"I have something for Cindy," Ethan said.

Normally I would have been super excited that Ethan McCallister was at my house, with something for me. But I was a skeleton so I really didn't care what he had. Even if it was the most amazing gift on the planet, I still would have wanted him gone.

"Why don't you come back tomorrow, Ethan?" Momster

said. Thank goodness she understood that I'd just DIE if he saw me as a skeleton!

I peeked around the couch and saw Ethan shaking his head. "I think Cindy would really like to see what I have."

"She can see it tomorrow," Dad said. "Come back first thing in the morning." He put his hand on Ethan's shoulder, guiding him toward the door, but Ethan resisted and neither one of them moved very far.

"Wait," Ethan said, his feet sliding on the floor as he tried to maneuver around Dad. His arms flailed. In his hand, there was something blue, but it was only a blur of color.

Dad stopped pushing and he got that look on his face where his mouth fell open and his eyes grew wide.

Ethan stopped flailing and the thing in his hand wasn't a blue blur anymore. It was clear as could be.

He held my blue Converse sneaker.

# chapter 29

Everyone gasped. At the same exact time.

Not only was Ethan holding my shoe, but I was so surprised I leapt up from behind the couch, revealing my skeleton self.

Right.

In.

Front.

Of.

Him.

All I wanted to do was grab the shoe out of his hands, and run to my room. I'd peek inside the shoe and if my boney skeleton foot was really there, I'd pull it out and stick it back on my leg. Unfortunately for me, it was only a little movie in my head. Instead, what I really did was stand there, frozen stiff, unable to move.

Ethan handed me the shoe. "I thought you might need this."

I peeked in and sure enough, my skeleton foot was inside.

If I wasn't a skeleton, I'm sure my heart would have pounded out of my chest. And if I had been normal-Cindy I would have probably looked like a slow motion clip from a movie where the person is making a really stupid face. But since I was a skeleton, I didn't have any expression. It was just all bone.

Then I realized the worst part of all.

He knew my secret!

I wanted to puke.

"It's okay," he said like he knew I was upset. Probably because it wouldn't take a genius to figure that one out.

"Um, yeah. I guess I kind of need that." I laughed nervously. I would have half-smiled if I had skin.

He half-smiled at me almost like he knew what I was thinking.

Before I could say "boo" (which would have been kind of funny since I was a skeleton and all) he sat down. Then something else occurred to me. Not only did he know my secret, he was still here.

He knew my secret and he was sticking around!

Ethan reached for my shoe. "So, can I, like, put it on for you?"

My eyes felt like they grew bigger and bigger as I watched him remove my skeleton foot from the sneaker. Then he bent down and snapped my skeleton foot back onto my skeleton leg.

"Well, there you go," he said so calmly that I wondered if there was something wrong with him.

But when I looked into his eyes, I knew it was all okay.

"So, Cindy," he said. "Can we finish that dance?"

I nodded like I'd become a major dork and couldn't say a single word.

### TIME OUT!

*Yes. I was speechless. It was one of the very few times in my entire skeleton-life that I couldn't say anything. I know you find that like kind of impossible. But yes, it's true. I can be quiet. Unlike you who keep asking questions. You're worse than my grandma. Do you think I can get back to the story now? 'Cause I'm almost done. Good. Thank you.*

Momster raced over to the counter and turned on the radio. The song "Do You Believe in Magic" floated through the air. Winnie and Bertha smiled as Ethan led me outside into the backyard. The moon was so full and bright it looked like I could reach out and touch it.

Ethan held my hand tight, but because I was a skeleton, there was no sweat pooling between our palms this time. We danced slowly, rocking back and forth to the music. At that same moment there was a loud howl. It was the same howl I'd heard when I hid in the bushes after I'd scared Mr. Peterkin. The same howl I'd heard when I counted my bones. Except this time it was loud, like it was right next to me.

My gaze darted around and I realized the sound came from Ethan.

But Ethan had changed. He was no longer cute, middle-schooler Ethan. He was hairy-werewolf Ethan.

*TIME OUT!*

*I did not see that coming. At all. Did you? If I hadn't been different, I probably would have run the other way. But since I was a skeleton, it wasn't a big deal that he was a werewolf. Until . . .*

Ms. Wanda came running across her backyard onto our patio. She stopped when she saw me dancing with Ethan and put her arm around Momster's shoulder. The two ladies exchanged hopeful smiles.

Happy, I smiled at Ethan. All of a sudden a picture flashed in my head. And I knew I recognized Ethan's doggie face. He was the same hairy mutt that chased me into the cemetery. "You're not going to eat my bones, are you?"

"Nope." He bared his teeth in a big smile. "Your bones aren't on the menu, remember?" Ethan tipped his head back and howled.

I burst out laughing. "Then why'd you chase me?"

"Just helping you find your way." He turned to Momster and Ms. Wanda, giving them both a big fanged smile.

Ms. Wanda waved her wand. "Needed all the help we could get, didn't we?"

An eyeball nearly popped out of my head. "You knew about this, too?"

"Sho' did, sugah." Cheddar scampered up Ms. Wanda's leg onto her shoulder. "Your momma did, as well."

My mom knew about it all. She'd asked for help. She didn't want me to feel alone. And I wasn't anymore. I clutched the key in my grip.

I tried to smile but my teeth just clanged together.

I turned toward Ethan, studying his furry face. It made me feel good to know that I wasn't the only one with a secret curse. So I didn't mind that he was different (especially since he wasn't going to gnaw on my bones and chew me up). In fact, I kind of liked him all "werewolfish." He definitely wasn't like any other boy I knew. And I bet that I wasn't like any other girl he knew.

Since we were sharing secrets, it was the right time to share my new name with him, too. "You can call me Cinderskella. What should I call you?" I wondered if he had a cool name like mine.

"Just call me the Big Bad Wolf." He howled.

When we went inside, Ethan spied the jar of pickled pigs' feet on the counter. "Mind if I have some? They're my favorite."

"Be our guest," we all said in unison.

"No more pigs' feet in this house. Unless of course, they're for you, Ethan." Dad slapped his hand against Ethan's back.

I knew that my dad had finally accepted me for who I was: freaky-cursed-skeleton-girl and average-middle-school-er-Cindy all wrapped up into one awesome kid.

When Ethan had polished off the jar of little piggy feet, he hugged me gently, being careful not to break my bones. "See you in school on Monday."

"Sure thing." I knew that I would never have to keep my secret a secret anymore. At least not from him. Or my family. And maybe I could finally share it with Sarah.

As soon as Ethan left, Momster grabbed a bag of marsh-mallows. "This calls for some s'mores."

"It sure does." Dad went outside and started a campfire.

Momster pushed a marshmallow onto the end of a stick. "I think my spell worked after all."

I knew exactly what she meant. Dad loved me for who I was and I wasn't ashamed of my secret. "It sure did."

"You know," my dad said once we were all seated around the fire. "I could get used to this."

I licked the sticky marshmallow off my boney fingers. "Me, too."

Dad wrapped his arms around me and squeezed until I couldn't bear it anymore.

"You're. Going. To. Break. Me," I gasped.

"Oh." He loosened his grip. "Sorry, Lovie."

I rolled my eyes around in my skull. "You're so weird."

Dad started laughing and so did I.

This was just the start of our new life together with Momster, Winnie, and Bertha. And more importantly, with Dad who loved me no matter what I looked like.

The rest of that night was filled with laughter as we told funny stories and I showed everyone the noises my bones could make. I also did my hand puppet games for them. The best part was I wasn't the only one laughing this time.

So that's my story. And normally, this is where I'd say, "And we all lived happily ever . . ." But who am I kidding? This is my life. Not a fairy tale.

# acknowledgements

The path to publication truly has been a roller coaster of emotions, and there are countless people who wiped my tears, answered too many emails, celebrated my victories, and happy-danced right along with me. I owe them a debt of gratitude.

First and foremost, many thanks to the members of my critique group, NI (Novel Idea). To Rose Cooper for being my BWFE (Best Writing Friend Ever) and laughing at my lame jokes. I'll try not to butt-dial you so often. To Judith Mammay for inspiring me to keep trying, to keep writing, and to never give up. Our talks forever remain engraved in my heart. To Ann Marie Meyers for believing in me. Luck would have us as crit partners, but perseverance would have us as publishing sisters—I'm happy to share this journey with you. To Mindy Alyse Weiss for her inspiration and vision of the Underworld. I'm so glad I listened to your advice.

Thank you to my beta readers, Laura Diamond, Casey Griffin and Daniel Rider. You guys rock! A huge round of applause to Mrs. Jones's fourth grade class (2009–10) for being the best test audience. Ever.

I'd be remiss if I didn't thank my awesome publishing and publicity team at Jolly Fish press. It's been a wild ride and I wouldn't have it any other way. A special thank you to Kirk and Christopher for your patience.

I'm grateful for my friends, near and far, for their support.

You know who you are. Thank you to all my cohorts, past and present, at my group blog, From the Mixed-Up Files of Middle-Grade Authors. It's been a fantastic experience working with each and every one of you and I'm so thankful for the friendships, support, and shared knowledge. Rock on middle-grade authors, rock on!

And to the online community of writers, you are what keeps the dream alive! Thank you.

To my family: My husband, Dr. Barry Borst, PhD (a.k.a. Ben Affleck) for believing in me when I didn't believe in myself; my daughters, Emily and Annelise for humoring my hours of reading aloud, acting goofy and driving them near batty with plot points and skeleton jokes. Thank you for still wanting to be associated with me even when it wasn't cool. Thanks to my parents, John and Roxanne, who are my personal cheerleaders. If this book is a success it's because my mother bribed people into purchasing it.

And of course, to my co-author and daughter, Bethanie, without whom this book would never have been written. Thank you for being awesome.

*Amie Borst*

Thank you to my elementary school librarian who ~~bored me~~ inspired me to write a fairy tale I'd actually want to read. Thanks Mom for writing all those query letters and finding Jolly Fish Press. Thank you Microsoft Wurd for fixing all my typos.

*Bethanie Borst*

# about the authors

**AMIE BORST**, a long-time writer and self-proclaimed graduate from ULE (University of Life Experience), is a native New Yorker, now residing in Northern Virginia. Originally, she aspired to be on Broadway, but her teen years were filled with too many "angsty" poems and short stories to let them fall to the wayside. She enjoys eating chocolate while writing and keeps a well-stocked stash hidden away from her family.

**BETHANIE BORST** is an all-rounder. She is a spunky 13-year-old who is an avid archer with Olympic dreams, enjoys the outdoors, loves reading and is quick to make lasting friendships. When she is not writing, she swings on a star.

Follow Amie and Bethanie on Facebook at:
facebook.com/AmieAndBethanieBorst

# about the illustrator

**RACHAEL CARINGELLA,** also known as Rachael Tree Talker, got her name from talking to trees when she was little. Drawing inspiration from daydreams and nightmares, folklore and fantasy, she is fascinated by all things dark and dreary, morbid and macabre, balancing them with the playful, happy, and the beautiful. She loves creepy trees and big mysterious eyes that tell stories. Rachael lives in a little house in the forests of Utah working as a full time artist with a dog, a cat, a collection of creepy clown dolls, and vintage gumball machines. She has pink hair, and currently blogs at:

talk2thetrees.com